SECRETS END

SECRETS END

RONALD HALE

S.I.T.E.
PUBLISHING

ISBN: 978-0-9796241-3-1
LCCN: 2023900161

This book is a work of fiction. Names, characters, places, and incidents are the product of the author's imagination or are used fictitiously. Any resemblance to actual events, locales, or persons, living or dead, is coincidental.

10 9 8 7 6 5 4 3 2 1

Printed in the United States of America

(Paperback) Second Edition: April 2023

SITE PUBLISHING
7330 Staples Mill Road #106
Richmond, VA 23228

Ronald Hale
ronhalebooks.com
sitepublishingtoday@gmail.com

Cover Design: JenC Designs

New to the SECRETS series?

*Enjoy all **three** books in the trilogy:*

SECRETS END (Book 1)

When criminal attorney Todd Banks uncovers a secret from his past, he finds himself questioning everything and everyone he knows. As he struggles to disentangle himself from an ever-expanding web of lies and betrayal, Todd discovers just how much his past has dictated his present.

SECRETS BEGIN (Book 2)

Growing up on the tough streets of Boston, where poverty and crime are the norm, and the only way out is in a body bag, prison or a miracle, fourteen-year-old Khalil Gilliam's life is turned upside down when a family secret is revealed.

Years later, he meets Todd Banks, a successful Boston attorney who reveals the truth about the secret buried years ago.

SECRETS ENEMY (Book 3)

With their family secrets already exposed, Todd and Khalil believe they are finally in the clear... until Khalil learns the lies he and Todd uncovered go deeper than either of them ever believed.

As they strive to reveal the truth once and for all, they discover just how deeply the lies and deceit have infiltrated their inner circle. Not everyone who smiles at you is happy to see you.

To Jesus Christ, my Lord and Savior.
The *greatest* influence in my life.

"Whom have I in heaven but you?
I desire you more than anything on earth."
Psalm 73:25

Prologue

GROWING UP IN the inner city of Boston, Massachusetts, poverty and crime were the norm. I didn't want to become another statistic like most of the guys in my neighborhood; they ended up in prison or dead. Instead, I took my destiny into my own hands. I exhausted most of my time on the blacktop, fine-tuning my basketball skills, or in the library, soaking up every book I could get my hands on. I believed wholeheartedly that "a mind is a terrible thing to waste."

I wanted to open the minds of the neighborhood thugs and playboys that there was more to life than just selling dope and impregnating the young girls in the hood. Though being young meant you got no respect in my parts, I believed if I could convince even one of my lost brethren, I would somehow change the minds of everyone in the hood.

As my academic prowess and skills on the blacktop grew, so did my reputation. Family and friends saw me as a cool, slightly militant kid with a surprising vocabulary that consisted of far more than ABCs and 123s. They eventually began dropping comments, alternately comparing me to Sidney Poitier and Malcolm X.

One icy winter day, Junior Walker, the neighborhood tough guy, rolled up on me as I was trying to recruit his younger cousin to my cause. Junior was as mean as a snake and built like the Incredible Hulk. He cornered me in the alley and demanded that I take my idiotic rhetoric out of the hood. "If I ever catch you preaching this pipe dream crap again, I'm going to set my foot so far up your ass, you're going to wish you were never born," he sneered.

"An 18 year old threatening an aspiring 11 year old community activist with violence doesn't seem wise," I said loftily, puffing out my chest just a bit.

"Community activist?" he barked, laughing menacingly in my face.

"If you don't take your little ass home and get the hell out of my face, my threat will come to fruition."

"Fruition is a great word. Where did you learn it?"

"Never judge a book by its cover, Shorty." He winked at his cousin. "What kind of kid are you anyway?" he spat, eyeing me over.

"The kind that wants to make a difference in the community." I reached inside my book bag. "Take a look at the strategic plan I put together last night. I believe you will find it very interesting."

"Didn't you hear what I just said, little ni...?" He slapped the literature out of my hand and violently squeezed the back of my neck.

I tuned out the rest of what he was saying. I'd learned long ago to ignore the derogatory word that people in our neighborhood used so frequently, as if there were nothing to it. However, if it originated from the mouth of someone outside our race, they were immediately primed to fight. Still, I'd learned that little of value ever came from it.

I tuned back in just in time to hear Junior wrap up his monologue. "We live in the gutter, and no one outside of these parts gives a damn about us. As soon as you realize this truth," he growled, releasing his vise-like grip on my neck, "come and see me, and I will give you a job."

"What kind of job?" I asked with skepticism, dusting off my literature. I rubbed the back of my neck, trying to ease the stinging.

"The kind that could get you killed," he grinned, then laughed as he walked away. Watching him saunter down the street, I knew he wouldn't live long.

I wasn't deterred. Day after day, I continued to frequent the library for brain food. By the time I was 12 years old, I had begun reading college-level books. I excelled at debating, challenging my teachers at every opportunity. I had big plans for myself, and I was on a mission to make my dreams come true.

Chapter 1

USING EVERY OUNCE of masculine strength, my hands tugged hard on the strap, tightening them on my backpack. Then my right hand stretched out to grab a hold of the Red Sox baseball cap from the hallway closet before reluctantly heading out. Looked like it was going to be another battle against the wintry New England wind. Turning to lock up, a sudden gust cut forcefully through the navy blazer and thin Lacoste sweater, sending icy shivers through every vein. Each limb was trembling now; I should have known better than to walk out of my apartment without a heavier coat, but no amount of cold was going to stand between me and my brand-new look.

Tucking in my chin from the wind and pulling high the neck of the sweater, a hurried pace was vital in the march toward Ashmont Station, determined to catch the 8:00 a.m. train to Harvard Square. There was no room for delay, not right now.

And soon, four blocks later, I had escaped the cutting cold, stepping into the heated station.

My hands fumbled, reaching inside the blazer for my wallet, ignoring the frozen stinging of my fingertips, searching for my train pass. Frustration was mounting.

Well dammit. I've left my pass in the coat I decided not to wear. What an idiot!

Teeth clenching, it was now necessary to head to the back of the line again to purchase a day pass. This was just too annoying, my body venting its accruing irritation by bumping into just about everyone along the way. Any semblance of good manners was by the wayside now.

The train would soon be pulling in, and my foot had a mind of its own, tap-tapping with anxiety. It wouldn't help matters at all; the line could only move ahead at its own pace, and nothing could get it to progress any faster. Still, my foot swung, and a sigh escaped.

The line inched forward, and now, that irksome woman behind was deliberately taking up my personal space, invading it, leaning ever so slightly against my sweater to say *hurry up, hurry up.* It wasn't sufficient pressure to say she shoved or pushed, but more than enough to indicate that she wanted to be in control of the pace at which the line moved. There really was no need.

We were moving forward, albeit slowly, and there was nothing I could do about the pace.

In the next second, I could feel her close to my body again, picking up the heat of her.

Taking a deep breath, I hurled my irritation toward the front of the line.

"What's the hold up?" I asked loudly.

From the front, a silver-haired woman rummaging through her purse mumbled, "It's in here somewhere." There was always one, always a pensioner who couldn't find their pass!

"Come on, lady," shouted an overweight, middle-aged white man. The light glinted off his receding hairline; he was apparently taking his cue from me, vexed and impatient.

It wasn't clear why his comment bothered me, especially since I'd just been so rude myself.

"Respect your elders, fat boy," my voice muttered. As if in defense of her, my feet were suddenly propelled toward the woman at the front of the line.

It was an excuse, a ruse if you like, a way to skip the long wait.

"Excuse me, ma'am," I greeted her warmly. "Let me help you out."

My gentlemanly facade would surely get me on that train. Turned out it wasn't her pass that she couldn't find; it was her money. And without that, she'd be heading nowhere.

"Oh, thank you so much, young man," she responded with a sincere smile. "I'm sure my money's in here somewhere," she said, digging deeper into her purse, her feeble hands slowing her progress. "I had some dollars. I know I did. I mean, I do. I must have."

The pockets of the purse came up empty. No wallet.

She appeared tearful and distraught now, most likely due to the mental pressure piling up from the queue of people unwilling to see the problem of being simply old and forgetful.

Maybe, just like me, she'd left what she needed at home, bringing the wrong purse out.

Suddenly, the train loomed in front of us, inciting a sense of panic in me. If I didn't act quickly, that train would come and go in the blink of an eye—without me aboard.

No way can I be late to work a second time this week.

"Not a problem at all," I said, offering a devilish smile while shoving her gently ahead of me to keep her moving forward. "I'm more than happy to pay your fare. To be honest, I came out today without my own rail pass so forgetting things is kind of second nature to me!"

Something in me wanted her not to feel so embarrassed. Now, she viewed me as an ally.

I quickly inserted my credit card to purchase two daily passes. Handing one ticket to the silver-haired woman, I rushed through the access gate, pushing only a few people aside and managing to squeeze onto the train as the doors slid shut. The elderly woman and the rest of those in the line were left there, still standing on the platform. It was clear she'd have liked to thank me for the kindness of the ticket but there wasn't time.

Her hand was outstretched as if to say, *wait a minute, I wanted to speak to you.*

Too late. At least the angry expressions also remained there, stuck, while I moved on and out of there. The train was pulling into its rhythm, gathering a pace too, picking up speed.

Indistinguishable but clearly hostile comments had floated in through the window as the train pulled away; everyone must have known I'd only paid the old lady's fare to cut the line.

"That was a close one." I spun around.

Wow! Now, I was facing a Zoe Saldana look-alike wearing a full-length cashmere coat over a stylish two-piece business suit.

"Almost missed it!" My face was almost cleaved in two by my inane and insincere grin.

"Well, that was a commendable thing you did for that poor woman." She smirked. "You're a real gentleman." Her words dripped with sarcasm. "Thank God men like you exist, huh?"

"Yeah, well, no one else seemed to want to help her out. No big deal." I shrugged, ignoring her judgmental remark though suddenly embarrassed by my pretentious behavior. It hadn't crossed my mind that my display might have drawn a larger audience.

"I guess chivalry isn't dead after all," she said in a lighter tone, her eyes playing chess with mine. "Mind if I ask you a question?" This woman did not seem to possess the snark of the first.

Hopefully, the spirit of my 'helping hands' had passed without this lady realizing the cause.

"Go for it," I responded, hoping my confident tone belied my embarrassment. Had she noticed me shoving the elderly woman? It seemed not. She appeared sincerely appreciative.

"Where are you from?" She asked with a raised eyebrow.

"Native Bostonian," I said. "Why do you ask?"

"Well, you seem like an intelligent man."

"I'd like to think so," I said, my confidence returning to match my tone. Was there some reason why a native Bostonian couldn't be smart?

"You're also exceptionally handsome and I like your sense of style." She openly looked me up and down.

"Thank you," I said, puffing up with pride. "You have that whole Vogue thing going on too." By this time, a number of on-lookers had begun blatantly eavesdropping on our conversation.

"Thank you." She nodded. "But you know what I've learned about all the good-looking, well-dressed guys in branded clothes?"

Ah. I should've anticipated there'd be more to that huge and unusual compliment. And she's about to expand on it in front of everyone. Well, damn.

"No, but why don't you enlighten me?"

I smiled and leaned forward, trying to look unfazed by her apparent interest.

"Are you sure your ego can handle it?"

"Try me," I replied, waiting for her next move.

"Well, it's the good-looking guys who always seem to have a screw loose if you know what I mean." She let out a small chuckle.

"Maybe." I smiled coyly. "But maybe, if women didn't drive men crazy, there'd be a few less screws in need of tightening—if you know what I mean."

There was a brief moment of silence and suddenly, we both laughed. She smiled. "I like that. You have a quick mind. Impressive."

"Yes, you are," I responded in a low tone, hoping she was feeling the same sudden attraction. It was odd to hear kind words because she plainly was not so impressed by my earlier behavior.

"I don't know if you watched the news this morning, but the meteorologist said we're in for one of the coldest winters New England's ever seen."

She looked me up and down once more, staring at my outfit.

I preened under her scrutiny.

"Yeah; heard something like that myself."

"So, what would make an intelligent man leave home in frigid temperatures without a coat?" She challenged, eyebrow cocked.

"Not going to lie to you. I didn't want to cover up my new outfit."

She tipped her head back and laughed louder this time, drawing more stares from our fellow passengers. "Oh my God!" She lost herself in uncontrollable laughter, also gazing around as if to see if anyone else had picked up on what she'd asked and the answer to it.

Her face said, *what a prize ass he is!*

"What's so funny?" I asked as if it wasn't crystal clear already.

"You've got to be kidding." She placed her hand over her mouth to muffle her laughter since she couldn't stop, only drawing more eyes to the pair of us.

"Are you seriously telling me the only reason you didn't wear a coat in the middle of winter is because you wanted everyone to see your outfit?"

"That's exactly what I'm telling you."

Without another word, she removed the scarf from around her neck and handed it to me.

"What's this for?" I asked.

"To keep you warm, city boy," she responded. "And to reward you for being honest."

"Thanks, I appreciate it."

She extended her hand. "My name is London."

I grabbed her warm hand as if it were a prized possession. "It's very nice to meet you, London. My name's Todd. And yes, I really do like my new sweater. Lacoste, in case you didn't know."

I turned my arm slightly, her fingers still in my gentle grasp. She still beamed.

My own smile tried to convey, *I'm not really a pretentious jerk.*

"It's a pleasure, Todd," she stated with a smile, revealing a perfect set of pearly whites.

"The pleasure is all mine," I assured her, reluctantly releasing her hand.

For the next few minutes, we rode the train in silence, sneaking sidelong glances at each other, smiling when caught.

"Harvard Square will be your next stop. Harvard Square," the sudden announcement boomed through the PA system, jolting me back to the present.

I shifted my backpack on my shoulders and met London's eyes again. "Well, as much as I hate for our conversation to end, Harvard Square is my stop."

"Well Todd, it was very nice meeting you." She smiled.

That's it? I thought. I wasn't ready to let her go, to allow the chemistry I hoped we both felt to slip through our fingers and disappear. I glanced around the car, scrambling.

What now? Ask for her number?

"How do I get this beautiful scarf back to you?" I blurted.

"No need," she said. "It's my gift to you."

That was emphatically not what I wanted to hear. She had missed her cue. My heart sank.

Now what? I thought, glancing around again.

An older white woman was staring up at me. "Ask her out," she mouthed silently as if her own life depended on it.

"London," I said hesitantly, wrenching my eyes back to hers again.

"Yes, Todd?"

"I'd like to return the favor. Is there a chance of seeing you again?" I stumbled over my words, hoping the awkwardness wasn't obvious. Just then, the screeching of brakes cut in, the train slowing as we pulled into Harvard Square.

"If it's meant to be, I won't be hard to find."

The train doors opened. I took a deep breath and half-heartedly stepped out.

"Phone number?" My back pressed forward into the train carriage, my mind doubting success.

"If the stars are aligned, we'll meet again," she assured me gently. It was final. That was all she would say on the matter, and she spoke like a judge. This was her verdict.

"Doors closing," blared through the train's speaker system.

Desperately, my voice blurted, "Will you at least give me your last name?"

Leaving my question hanging in the air, she smiled, and this was all she was prepared to offer. "I hope we meet again, Todd."

Her eyes held mine as the doors slid shut. "Checkmate," they seemed to say, and my psyche felt as if I'd lost the game and the prize all at once.

The train pulled away and with a sigh, I turned to leave the station.

Chapter 2

HEADING OUT OF Harvard Square, my head reeled as if I had just thrown away the winning Mega Millions ticket. Thoughts spun. *What if the stars don't align again? What if it's just not meant to be? What if everything that could be never is?*

I sighed, slipping London's soft and scented scarf inside my bag.

Now joining the crowds of Cambridge, it was a case of fighting through the people to reach my office, a world champion boxer on his way to the ring. The crowds seemed to follow me everywhere as if to show me up for all the cringe-worthy behavior of earlier in the day.

Finally, at 8:45 a.m., I stepped through the glass doors of my office building.

London had still not gone away, lingering heavy in my mind.

"Good morning, Todd," voiced Officer Jackson, the only female security guard for the building. She shot me a bright smile, then headed my way with open arms.

"Are you okay?" She asked, throwing her arms around my neck, latching onto me like a pit bull. "You smell great," she whispered softly, drawing curious stares. No doubt she was catching the wonderful scent of the woman's scarf that nestled atop all my belongings. Or it could have been my cologne, some of which must have worked its way into the soft sweater fabric.

"Yeah, I'm good." Quickly, my body worked to free itself from her grasp, heading toward the elevator before her antics scored me a spot on the office gossip list.

Stepping into the elevator, I turned to select my floor, spotting notorious office gossip Wendy Wilson rushing toward me. "Hold the elevator!" she called.

Oh, hell no. I backed farther inside, mashing the 'close door' button repeatedly. "Close door, close!" Finally, they began to slide shut. Mission accomplished!

It was worth a celebration as they snapped closed in Wendy's face.

"Looks like someone is in a hurry," rang out a female voice already in the elevator.

She was attractive, sharply dressed, green-eyed, with curly red hair.

"Um, yeah, sort of," I lied.

"What's the rush?"

"Running late for my nine o'clock meeting."

"Oh, I see." She placed her hands on her hips. "So, you don't think the woman asking you to hold the elevator for her was running late too?"

"I don't know," I said, embarrassed. *Oh crap. Talk about landing myself in it. How many times in one day can I make these screw-ups?*

"Which floor?" She barked rudely.

"27."

"27?" She said. "Then you must be Todd Banks, the firm's newest recruit."

"You've heard of me then." I was feeling accomplished.

"Of course." She extended her hand. "Your reputation precedes you. Everyone's heard of Todd Banks, the wonder boy. It's nice to finally meet you."

"Finally meet me?" I responded with skepticism.

"Yes. My name is Amanda Pizzo, of Pizzo and Associates

and I'm the prosecuting attorney who plans to sink your client, William 'The Titanic' Gammon."

My wits escaped me momentarily.

"Can I ask you a question, Attorney Banks?" She pressed.

"Do I have a choice?" I joked.

"What reputable firm would knowingly represent murderous, low-life, drug-dealing thugs?"

Before I could respond, the elevator came to a stop and the doors slid open. But the answer would've been *every criminal law firm would, that's what.* Without offering offenders a solid defense, trials floundered, and a mistrial could result. Yet people still held these blinkered views.

Of course, fellow attorneys knew all this, but this woman was just trying to irritate me.

"Enjoy your day, wonder boy." She stepped out, then turned and smiled. It appeared disingenuous. "See you in court."

The elevator continued to the 27th floor. As it stopped and the doors slid open, I exited to the right, headed down the corridor and stopped at the desk of Judy Morrison, office paralegal. As usual, she was packing on the makeup.

"Good morning, Judy."

"Good morning, Mr. Banks," she clamored with excitement. "You're looking particularly handsome today."

I ignored her comment, now unsure if any female could be taken at her word or whether this might open the latest door to a fresh insult for me. I was a slow learner but at least did learn.

"I need you to pull the Gammon files for me as soon as possible."

"Sure thing, Mr. Banks!"

"Also, cancel all of my appointments for the day. I just ran into the prosecuting attorney for the Gammon case and she's on the warpath."

"I'm on it."

"Thank you, Judy."

"You're welcome, Mr. Banks."

"One more thing, Judy," I said, turning.

"Yes, Mr. Banks."

"Will you please stop calling me Mr. Banks?"

"Yes, Mr. Banks… I mean Todd." We laughed in unison as I headed into my office.

Attorney Pizzo was right about Gammon: He was a known felon with mafia ties. This time around, he'd been charged with racketeering and first-degree murder, allegedly having shot a whole family of three execution-style, then he'd burned the house down with them inside.

Despite the overwhelming evidence against him, it was my job to prove that my client was not guilty beyond a reasonable doubt. It was going to be an uphill battle.

****

Around 6:00 p.m., the workday was done and a cold beer called, as well as a Black & Mild cigar and an urge to see London again. Even after hours of intensive case review, she still felt close by.

The connection of this morning was real, wasn't it? Not just a chance meeting on the train. For a moment, my mind spiraled, bringing thoughts of the kiss we had yet to share.

Shaking myself out of the daydream, I shoved my files in a drawer, locked up the office and headed toward the elevator.

The elevator doors slid open, and I made my descent to the first floor.

When the doors opened, there stood Mr. Burke, another one of the office security guards, clearly on evening duty.

"Attorney Banks," he said smiling.

"Hey, Mr. Burke." I forced a smile. "How are you?"

"Blessed and highly favored," he chuckled back.

"Can I ask you a question, Mr. Burke?"

"Sure."

"Why do religious people always say they are blessed and highly favored?"

He rested a hand on my shoulder and steered me around the corner toward the reception desk. "When individuals commit their lives to Christ," he explained with great seriousness. "Then—and only then—are they considered blessed and highly favored. As followers of Christ, we are no longer held hostage by sin."

"Oh, right." I was wishing I'd never asked. "Well, that sounds pretty nice, but I don't know anyone who doesn't have an issue or two."

"Listen," he said, removing his hand from my shoulders and making his way behind his desk without seating himself. "I'm a sinner saved by grace."

He stated it as if his answer explained everything.

"With all due respect, Mr. Burke, you're preaching to the wrong one. I don't go to church, and don't read the Bible." Hopefully, this cold declaration would end our discussion.

"What do you know about Jesus?" He challenged, leaning to rest his elbows on his desk.

"My mother and grandmother are devout Christians and they dragged me to church for years. But these days, I don't believe in anyone or anything that I can't see."

"Then you are a damn fool!" he barked, drawing out the cry of *damn*, and slamming one hand down hard on the desk. Clearly, my words must have struck a nerve.

"Who do you think woke your lazy ass up this morning?" He shouted.

"Who and what I believe in is my business," I shot back. "I woke myself up this morning. Same as I do every morning. Have a good night, Mr. Burke."

"I'm going to pray for you, Attorney Banks. I'm going to pray to save you."

"Pray for your damn self," I tossed back, turning to leave.

"You need Jesus, you young punk!" he declared.

Before I could get far, Wendy Wilson walked up.

"Hey, Wendy," I said quickly, glad for the interruption.

"How are you?" She asked.

"I'm doing well," I said. "Just chatting with Mr. Burke about life."

"Any interesting epiphanies?"

"Nothing you would be interested in," I deflected.

I thought, *actually, nothing I was much interested in either.*

"Well, Mr. Banks," Mr. Burke said sternly. "We'll continue our discussion another time."

"Great."

Relieved to have the conversation with Mr. Burke behind me, I made my way out of the office park, back toward Harvard Square.

Chapter 3

AT THE HARVARD Square train station, a large crowd had amassed at the center of the platform, waiting for the train. A shabby looking gentleman with long dreadlocks eyed me, dressed in a wrinkled black, yellow and green Bob Marley T-shirt and dark sunglasses. He was whistling the Bob Marley classic, 'No Woman, No Cry'.

"What's going on?" He spoke with a heavy accent, maybe Jamaican or Trinidadian. He definitely wasn't a northerner.

"Same thing, different day," I answered pitifully.

"Why the long face?" He asked.

It was a damn good question, and one I couldn't answer even

with thirty-one years under my belt. "Just had a long day," I said, raising the corner of my mouth in a half smile as I scanned the crowded station, hoping to spot London. It was hard to believe it had been less than ten hours since we'd met; it felt as though I'd known her forever.

"What's your story?" I asked the man, hoping to turn the conversation away from myself.

"I'm a freelance photographer," he said with pride. "Would you like to see some of my award-winning work?"

"Sure." I had a few minutes until the train arrived anyways.

He removed a high-tech digital camera from his carrier bag and began to share recent images.

"You're good," I said. "Really good."

"Thanks."

I handed him my business card. "My name is Todd."

"My friends call me Rasta," he said, closely examining my card. "You're really an attorney?" He looked up at me with eyes wide.

"Yes." I chuckled. "Haven't you ever met an attorney before?"

"Not a black one."

"Well, there are lots of us out here," I assured him. "And I'm just a regular guy with a job."

"A damn good job," he said and laughed as the train loomed into the station.

Fifteen minutes into the ride home, the commuter-packed train began to empty, so I grabbed a seat next to a young Hispanic girl wearing a form-fitting SpongeBob T-shirt and skinny jeans. She was cradling a small, screaming child.

"I'm sorry," she apologized to the passengers on the train who'd been shooting her annoyed looks. "Shhh…" She gently rubbed the top of the baby's head and rocked him back and forth.

"Whatcha starin' at, ya bumbaclots?" Rasta called out at the passengers. "Rude boy, bumbaclots," he repeated, shaking his head.

He met my eyes, and I shook my head at him.

Leaning in close to the young mother and me, he whispered without a hint of an accent, "I'm not really from Jamaica, but I have been studying the language and culture for years!"

At this, the three of us began to laugh.

"Everything is going to be okay," I said to the young girl, treating her like a younger sister.

"Thank you." She smiled tentatively.

"Do you mind if I take a few pictures of you and your beautiful child?" asked Rasta. His accent was back in place.

"I don't mind," she shifted the baby in her arm and turned to smile for the camera.

As Rasta snapped away, again my thoughts drifted to my interlude with London. I had no way of reaching her. Would I ever see her again or would my life simply continue, one day after the next, until she eventually faded and became nothing more than a distant memory?

That thought twisted my gut, so I quickly erased it from my mind.

"Fields Corner will be your next stop. Fields Corner," announced the conductor through the PA system. Perfect time for an interruption, I thought.

"Fields Corner is my stop," the young mother said, smiling.

Rasta handed me his camera as he and the young woman exchanged information so he could send her the pictures. With nothing to add to their conversation, I decided to be nosy, scrolling through the pictures he'd taken. I flipped through a bunch of the young mother and her child before hitting his older images. Suddenly, one caught my eye.

"What the…" I zoomed in on an image. "Rasta, who is this?"

I pointed at the small screen.

He glanced over. "Oh, I don't know. An actress from a photoshoot I did the other day." He turned back to the young woman.

"What's her name?" I asked excitedly.

"What's whose name?" He turned toward me again.

"The actress whose picture you took. What's her surname? You must know it."

"Hm… I don't know." He shrugged. "She's just someone who got in the photograph, you know. Hell, I take a lot of… and if I asked them all for their names… oh boy."

He was way more interested in the pictures he was taking right now and couldn't even be bothered to complete most sentences. But you could've scraped my jaw up off the ground.

Moments later, the train was slowing, pulling into Fields Corner.

As Rasta and the young Hispanic mother stood, I handed his camera back, sighing.

"What is her name? I need to know her name!"

They smiled and waved, disembarking as the train doors slid closed. It was too late.

I slumped in my seat, defeated.

As the train prepared to leave the station, my thoughts spiraled back to the wonderful encounter earlier that morning. Suddenly, a loud bang assaulted the train window. Rasta.

Hands cupped around his mouth, he shouted, "Marcelle! Her name is Marcelle!"

The train pulled away and I sighed. I'd held out hope for a moment, but it looked like I was headed home with no London and no leads. *Same old, same old*, I thought.

Who was I kidding, thinking I'd randomly cross paths with the same person twice in one day? Boston was a big city. This woman in the images couldn't have been the same one because her name sure wasn't Marcelle.

Chapter 4

IT WAS 5:00 A.M. on Sunday morning when my body somehow rolled out of bed and headed to the patio, snagging a Corona to sip as I watched the sun rise.

Watching the dawn while drinking a brew brought instant gratification; it was the only time of ever feeling at one with the world. The simplicity of a beer at daybreak took me away from the stresses of life and there sure were plenty of those.

As the sun's rays crept over the horizon and stained the sky, the cool morning breeze caused the hairs on my arms to stand on end. Deciding this refreshing start to the day deserved another beer, I stepped inside, grabbing my second Corona and heading back out to the patio.

Twenty minutes later, I headed back indoors feeling slightly buzzed.

The fridge promised another beer, but the ring of the cell phone intervened.

It was my boy and frat brother, Blake Harden.

"Top of the morning, TB," he shouted in my ear.

"What's up, Blake?" I replied, pulling the phone away from my head to keep him from bursting my eardrum.

"Today's the day, man. Last month while we were out drinking at the Violet Lounge, you agreed to attend church service with me for Family and Friends Day. Well, this is it, bruh."

"No way." I closed the refrigerator door. "You're lying."

"Maybe you don't remember because you were drinking tequila shots when I asked. But you said you would roll with me, so get up and meet me at the church. I'm texting you the address."

"But I'm not a Christian," I protested. "I don't believe all that Bible rhetoric."

"Just texted you the address. See you soon, man!" Before I could reply, Blake hung up.

Tossing my phone on the bed, I dropped to the edge of the

mattress. My face was resting comfortably in my hands. The questions poured free.

"Todd, why did you ever let this fool talk you into going to church? That's what you get for being a people pleaser. Now, you have to sit in church for hours, listening to a boring sermon."

Pulling myself to my feet, I shook it off and reluctantly grabbed my beige two-piece suit and freshly dry-cleaned white shirt from the bedroom closet. But rather than getting dressed, I plopped back down on the edge of the bed, racking my brain.

What's a good reason to skip church? C'mon, man, there must be hundreds.

Any strokes of brilliance escaped me but the Bible that my mother had given me as a child was staring at me from across the room. That thing was more a sentimental decoration than any kind of statement about my beliefs, but despite its dusty cover, it still held a certain allure.

Seeing it made me hustle to the shower to freshen up.

An hour and one deep breath later, my lips were blowing the accumulated dust off my Bible. Now, I was intent on heading out, though still trying to figure out how to get out of my commitment and reclaim those three hours about to be lost, ones I'd never get back once they were spent. Hell, didn't people say life was too short?

And wasn't it God who was reputed to decide when it was time to call us to death anyway? Seemed He was responsible for everything, whether the do-gooders were admitting to it or not.

It was impossible to win, then. Finally admitting defeat, I turned the radio to the local Gospel station to put me in a churchy mood.

It didn't work out, only seeming to depress me more, so with a single click, I killed the gospel choir, instead opening up my glove compartment to grab an old-school rap CD and my opened pack of Black & Mild cigars. Before too long, the fat cigar was in my hands and lit, and the window was down. EPMD's classic hit, 'Just like Music' was telling the neighborhood the black attorney was on the move again, off to God only knew where.

"Yeah, that's more like it," I said with a smile, leaning back and nodding my head to the beat.

A few minutes later, the car was pulling into the church's parking lot which offered everything from rag-top Porsches to broken down hoopties.

It was something of an art form to avoid getting your car scratched in this place, so I carefully parked between an antique-styled Mercedes and a jet-black Cadillac Escalade with gold rims.

Blake's car, however, was nowhere in sight, so my fingertips danced across the phone's handset to call him before walking inside.

"Hello?" a groggy voice answered.

"Blake, please don't tell me you're still in bed. That is not what I want to hear."

"My bad, T.B. Must have drifted back off." He yawned loudly. "What time is it?"

"It's 10:45," I said with an attitude. "The time you said we were meeting at church."

"Slow it down, pretty boy," he said, laughing. "I'll be there before the service is over."

"I can't believe I let you set me up."

"How else was I going to get you to church?" he joked. "Look, just go inside and enjoy the service. Besides, you didn't come out to church to see me anyway, did you?"

"You're wrong, man. Dead wrong."

"Well, you'll thank me later," he promised. "Call me after church, all right? Tell me what the sermon's all about."

"What happened to 'I'll be there before service is over?'"

"I'm a lawyer," he laughed. "I lied. You shoulda known."

I ground my teeth. "And what will God think of you not

showing up to church on Family and Friends Day after you promised you'd be there?"

"As I have stated a million times before… God knows my heart. He forgives me for everything."

"Typical response from someone trying to get out of a commitment."

"Just call me after church, okay?"

"Yeah, whatever." He couldn't see it, but I shook my head anyway.

"Peace, TB."

"Peace, Blake."

Taking a deep breath and grabbing the small Bible from the passenger seat, I heaved myself out of my car. It felt too wrong to just abandon the church after already making such an effort to be here, so my doubts had to be suppressed.

At the entrance, I was popping Altoids as if they were downers.

Entering the main sanctuary, an attractive, athletic woman with black hair and ocean-blue eyes greeted me. "Good morning, brother." She smiled. "It's so good to see you."

It wasn't evident why seeing me was good today; my face sure wasn't a picture of delight.

"Good morning," I said cautiously, also skeptical about her 'brother' remark. Was she referring to me being black, or did she think I was a believer?

"This way." She pointed. "Is this your first time visiting our church?"

"Yes, it is." What had she meant by the term 'brother?'

"Awesome! You will truly enjoy the service."

Oh, I doubt it, went the little voice inside my head.

"Thanks." The corner of my mouth rose in a half-smile as I took my seat in the second pew and placed my Bible down on the seat next to me, trying to get comfortable. Looking up a moment later, an elderly gentleman stared at me from the other end of the pew.

It seemed he was looking right through me, and it made me uncomfortable.

"How are you doing, sir?" I asked politely. What I really wanted to know was why the old fool was giving me the side-eye as if I was going to rob the church.

"It looks like someone got up on the wrong side of the bed," he whispered. "Have you been drinking today?" He moved closer to me as though thinking it was his duty to smell my breath.

"Drinking?" His accusation, though accurate, made me

defensive. "What makes you think I've been drinking?" I boomed, hoping the elevated bass in my voice would intimidate him.

"Lower your tone, son!"

Before he could say another word, I surreptitiously slipped a few more clutched Altoids into my mouth. To avoid drawing any more attention, the humble route was more fitting.

"I apologize if I offended you, sir. Would you happen to know what the word of the day is?" At his mercy, I grasped for an alternate topic of conversation, unsure of what else to say.

"The word is Jesus!" he said with a booming bass but an unimpressed stare.

"Jesus is a very good word." I grimaced. "When does service begin?"

"Whenever the Holy Spirit shows up."

"Well, I sure hope the Holy Spirit shows up soon," I whispered under my breath, hoping he didn't hear me.

"Are you sure you haven't been drinking?"

His probing was starting to get to me. Now, my eyes were scanning the room for the quickest exit. If there was no escape from this crazed maniac soon, I was afraid of cracking under the pressure. Then, all eyes in the church would be on me, no thanks to the Holy Spirit.

With no quick exit in sight, my head bowed, my eyes falling gently closed, all the while just hoping the cantankerous old man would assume the power of prayer had claimed me.

Though I didn't think any odor was possible with the number of Altoids I'd consumed, my devout positioning also gave a chance to blow into my hands to check for a beer stench.

Midway through my self-made breathalyzer, a beautiful sound drifted to my ears, a modern-day Marvin Gaye singing the most amazing rendition of 'Now Behold the Lamb' by Kirk Franklin and the Family. The pre-service music had begun with some serious style.

My eyes searched for the face of the gifted singer.

To my surprise, the voice belonged to a freckle-faced Ed Sheeran look-alike.

"Sing it, Sam," shouted a well-dressed woman seated in the front pew.

Even the old man who'd come down hard on me was jamming to the music. His face had somehow softened and now appeared almost angelic. Maybe I had been wrong about him. Maybe he was a good guy. Perhaps I was the one who needed to loosen up.

Bobbing my head and tapping my feet, the choir shifted to Tasha Cobbs' hit song 'Happy.' The music began to take me and for the first time all morning, church reached my soul, and a wide smile passed across my face. When the pace of the music picked up, I set free the top button on my shirt and loosened my tie. The music was moving me and before long, I was dancing in the aisle, doing the Milly Rock and the Dab at the same time.

I was having such a good time dancing that I didn't even realize the old man was staring at me with a what in the world are you doing, look on his face.

At once, I retook my seat in an effort to save myself from further embarrassment.

"Thank you, Jesus," shouted a brown-skinned woman with tears in her eyes. "Thank you, Jesus!" she repeated over and over.

"Amen." The word was just for show, to impress the old man. "God is good." I glanced down the pew to see if he'd noticed, but he was too busy watching the choir wrap up their final notes.

After the choir exited the stage, a short, stocky, dark-skinned man in an oversized suit stepped up to the lectern and grabbed the microphone.

"Good morning, saints," he boomed.

"Good morning!" everyone shouted in unison.

"This is the part of our service where we welcome all first-time visitors. Do we have any first-time visitors here today?"

Now, my body was motionless and rigid there in the pew, willing invisibility on myself.

But the old man piped up.

"Ohhh yes! We have a new visitor right here!" he announced, pointing at me.

I ground my teeth, but shot the old man a small, half-hearted smile.

"Stand up, son," the old man encouraged loudly.

Slowly, I traced my index finger down the side of my face and rose to my feet.

"We would like to thank you for visiting our church today," the man behind the mic said. "Please make yourself at home and let the Holy Spirit lead you."

I only wish the Holy Spirit would lead me out of this place!

But as my thought passed through my mind, a thunderous roar of applause emanated from the congregation. Some people were on their feet clapping, all looking my way. Embarrassment?

It was wonderful—divine, perhaps!

Surprised, I raised my hand in return, waving. "Thank you. Thank you so much."

The warm reception touched me. I continued greeting and thanking those nearby when out of the corner of my eye, I caught sight of the old man heading my way. Covertly, I placed my hand over my mouth and blew. *Please don't let him tell me I smell like beer again,* I thought.

"Greetings once again," he said, smiling for the first time all morning. "My name is Russell Chandler."

"Good morning, Mr. Chandler." I extended my hand, relieved that his scrutiny seemed over. "My name is Todd Banks."

"It's a pleasure, Todd." He gripped my hand firmly. Since the start of service, Mr. Chandler's entire demeanor had shifted. His eyes were no longer cold and callous, but vibrant and clear, his earlier flint-like tone replaced with love and kindness. I could only figure this was what he'd meant when he said we were waiting for the Holy Spirit to arrive.

"Welcome to the church," he continued. He grasped my hand in both of his.

"Thank you." To my own surprise, the smile would not leave my lips, and was sincere this time. "I appreciate the warm welcome. I'm truly honored."

But the continued warm hugs and smiles from this room full of strangers rendered me vulnerable, weak, humble—and perhaps a shadow of my usual self.

"Thank you," I repeated over and over. Finally, the stocky man reclaimed the microphone and invited the crowd to settle, so I took my seat, overwhelmed by a slew of emotions.

They came coursing through me, throwing me off balance.

I thought I'd known what church was all about. At any rate, mother and grandmother had dragged me there on plenty of occasions as a child. But the black church was all I'd known, and this sanctuary held little resemblance to my childhood memories.

Gone were the older black women wearing long white dresses and white gloves, standing like sentinels to greet those entering the sanctuary.

In my memories, there had never been a white face in the house unless it was election time, the politicians playing every card to try to win black votes. Yet right in front of me were people from all nations praising and worshipping together. Every person here was celebrating a Jesus who, despite spending years rejecting him, I was suddenly craving and longing to know.

Snapping me back to the present, a sultry, "Good morning, saints," echoed through the room.

Now, a stunning woman was standing tall behind the pulpit.

She oozed power and confidence and as sunlight poured into the sanctuary through the church's many windows, it almost seemed as if her presence lit up the room.

As her godly presence spread through the church and captivated the congregation, her face drew me more closely.

A curious familiarity quickly washed over me. I blinked and squinted. Was it…? "No way," I whispered. It surely couldn't be. My heart rate jumped up.

"Excuse me, Mr. Chandler," came my stuttering tone, trying to keep my voice down and the excitement out of my voice. "But who is she?"

"That's Pastor Patterson."

"Mr. Chandler, would her first name happen to be London?"

Before he could open his mouth to respond, his eyes had given me my answer.

No. It wasn't.

Chapter 5

THOUGH STILL APPRECIATING the touching welcome that had kicked off the service, it didn't take long before it came back to me why church wasn't a regular part of my week anymore. Staring at Pastor Patterson all morning proved to be an unexpected perk, but I still found myself wishing to hear her name was London, just as my brain had told me for one brief, hopeful moment.

But this was not London, and now, the sermon was dragging painfully.

Plus, why did they have to pass their collection plate around three times?

What the hell was a *love offering*, anyways?

The arduous service had left me drained and on edge, my restless foot prone to tapping impatiently as several laypeople wrapped up the service by announcing upcoming church events.

My emotions had cooled now. The joy was gone already, the excitement, the heady way in which my soul had discovered the glory and grace of praising God again.

Now, in its place, was nothing greater than an anxiety, an anxiousness to escape these wannabe religious zealots pretending to be cool with a total stranger. *It's unbelievable they pulled me in like that. I'm so damn gullible.* Finally released from our seats, I kept my eyes down and my chin tucked in, making a dash toward the exit, hoping to avoid the meaningless charade of after-church chit-chat and the inevitable matadors ready to latch on.

They were coming to convert me soon—as usual. Well, what else would they do? That was how things always went after church services, wasn't it? Show me a church any different.

This was not on the menu for me, not now, and not ever. Instead, a cold brew and a Black & Mild would be just the ticket to take the edge off and help me leave this whole experience.

"Have a great day," warbled an elderly woman in a bright red hat.

"Thanks," I said, barely glancing at her as I brushed by without slowing my pace.

Just a few more steps and I'll be free, I thought, pushing open the sanctuary doors and excitedly crossing into the church lobby.

"Free at last, free at last, thank God Almighty I am free at last!"

My gaze lifted to find the exit, but now, they suddenly met the blue-eyed greeter who had walked me into the sanctuary earlier. "My good brother," she greeted now, standing directly in front of me as other parishioners passed us by.

Without warning, she grabbed me by the hands, nestled close enough to kiss me and stared deep into my eyes. "Did you enjoy today's worship service?"

What the hell? Let go of my hands before someone sees us, I thought, managing to free one by swiftly pulling back and casting a serious look her way. But she stared on as if intent on mesmerizing me. "It was a very nice service." A bogus smile curved my lips, the same kind of smile a traveling salesman learns to use. "Very much enjoyed it."

"That is awesome, Brother. Um… What is your name again?"

"Again?" I didn't remember telling her. "It's Todd. Todd Banks."

"Brother Banks," she repeated as she shifted her grip to the back of my tricep, squeezing tightly. She did not bother introducing herself. "Someone works out," she added instead.

Then she winked, flashing her pearly whites as she slipped her other hand back into mine.

"Yeah, a little." I felt as if the entire congregation was watching.

"So, Brother Banks, will we be seeing you at church next Sunday?"

"Hell no," I wanted to say—shout, in fact—the gentlemanly approach seemed better. "If it's God's will, then you will see me."

My words reminded me of London's, to me: *If the stars are aligned... If it's meant to be...*

"When it concerns the Kingdom of God, it is always His will," she pressed.

"Yeah, if you say so," I responded, poker-faced and sick of having an earful about God.

"Well, do you have other plans more important than worshipping our precious Lord and Savior?" She watched me like a hawk, her beady eyes moving just like those of a bird of prey.

"Um, I won't know till I check my calendar, but don't be surprised if you see me next week."

"Great, so we'll see you next week then."

"But I do still have to check my calendar."

What part of that didn't she understand?

"Again," she said with a half-smile. "What could be more important than God?"

What kind of question was that? "I don't know."

"You don't know?"

Her eyebrows raised with concern. "Why don't we ask Mr. Chandler what he thinks is more important than worshipping God?" Her face lit up.

Mr. Chandler was escorting a well-dressed older woman and heading straight for us.

Damn, I thought, finally freeing my sweaty palms from her grasp and wiping them on the back of my pants.

"Brother Banks," he boomed.

"Hey, Mr. Chandler."

"I'm sorry that Pastor Patterson didn't turn out to be who you thought she was, but you are making friends already, huh? See! Lose one thing, and our bountiful Lord provides anew."

"Yeah, this good lady was just asking how I enjoyed the service and if I plan to visit again," I responded hurriedly, feeling the sweat beading on my forehead. Why that topic had slipped from my tongue was unclear; it would have been better to avoid it for the foreseeable future.

"Brother Banks says he has to look at his calendar in case he has something more important to do next week… preventing him from committing to God."

There was a tone of exasperation and no doubt a hidden eye roll in her statement.

I never said that, you blue-eyed devil! I thought, clenching my teeth.

"Can you think of anything or anyone more important than God, Mr. Chandler?" she continued, smiling fiendishly at me.

"Is that what Brother Banks thinks?" he said, resuming the flint-like stare he'd unleashed on me before service. "Please tell me that you do not believe anything or anyone is more important than our precious Lord and Savior. A man would have to be struck dead by lightning before he cannot attend church. But I am sure this is just a misunderstanding."

"My friend and I may have plans to watch the football game next Sunday."

For once, I opted for honesty, sick and tired of playing this religious game. "If I am not in church next week, that will most likely be the reason." There, I'd said it.

Their looks were unamused. Serious and stark.

"Cancel those plans immediately and make sure you are in

church next Sunday, Brother Banks!" His admonishment was laughable, but my demeanor managed to keep a serious look.

My mouth longed to respond with a "hell no" but the gathering of churchgoers surrounding me emphasized I should never forsake a meeting with the Body of Christ. I had understood this to be a conversation with the blue-eyed temptress and Mr. Chandler, but apparently word spread quickly in this place. A slight toward the Lord was a grievous offense to every person here.

I fended off the crowd as best I could, promising a life of eternal servitude in my haste to escape the onslaught. Finally, I exited the church building, once again emotionally drained.

I wasn't sure of having made much of a case for never returning.

As Jay-Z said, "I have 99 problems..." And now the church was one more.

"Brother Banks? Brother Banks!" Blue-eyes was calling to me, exiting the building.

What now? I stood still, watching her approach.

As she sauntered forward, she reached up and removed a white clip that held her dark hair neatly in a bun, allowing it to tumble gracefully down the middle of her back.

"Can I ask you a question?" She smiled, running one hand

through the dark strands while releasing the top button of her blouse with the other.

"Sure," I replied cautiously. After the way she had thrown me under the bus in front of Mr. Chandler and the others, not a word coming out of her mouth was to be trusted.

Having said that, the sex appeal she was exuding seemed most enjoyable.

"I don't know how to ask you this." She tilted her head coyly. "But here goes nothing. Would you like to go out for a cup of coffee sometime?"

I raised my eyebrow at her. "Like on a date or something?" I asked suspiciously.

"No, silly," she said, playfully jabbing me in the arm. "I just would like to have a cup of coffee with my brother in Christ. Is there anything wrong with that?"

"Hmm." My knuckles traced down the side of my jaw in an attempt to buy myself a moment. Then my gaze came back up to face her, trying to keep my eyes away from her cleavage, seeking to focus on our talk. "Nothing wrong with that at all."

But why had she singled me out and continued to refer to me as her brother in Christ when I had never accepted Jesus Christ as my Lord and Savior? Only she could know.

"Oh, forgive me, Brother Banks. I'm so sorry."

"For what?" I asked, confused.

"You're seeing someone, aren't you?"

"Huh, what?" My thoughts jumped to London and unexpectedly, my heart fell. "No, I am single in every sense of the word." I sighed, wishing I could tell her otherwise.

"Not for long," she whispered under her breath.

"What did you say?" I inquired, pretending I hadn't heard.

"I didn't say anything. So we have a date then?"

"Date?" Skepticism tinged my voice. "I thought we were just having coffee as brother and sister in Christ, weren't we?" I would play a game with her if she wanted it that way.

And I'd be sure to win it, too.

"Yeah, that's what I meant," she said, giggling like a schoolgirl.

"Okay, that's cool."

Against my better judgment, it seemed we had just arranged a date—a date featuring one of the unlikeliest couples ever. In my thirty-one years on Earth, I had never been interested in, attracted to, or even considered doing anything with a white woman, including having a cup of coffee. However, here was one in front of me and an attractive one at that.

So, here was a dilemma, a dichotomy, an inconsistency in

myself. *I am not attracted to white women. But hell, she's attractive. In what world does that make any sense?*

I shrugged to myself. *Why not now? Maybe my views have changed.*

With London nowhere to be found, there was nothing to lose.

"Here's my number." She handed me a pale pink napkin that let off a light, sweet fragrance. "Call me."

"Okay." I slipped the scented napkin inside my pants pocket.

So in a short period of time, I had accrued a scented scarf and now, a scented napkin to join it. I would soon need a bigger bag at this rate.

"It was so nice meeting you today, Todd," she enthused, throwing her arms around my neck and embracing me tightly.

Moments later, I watched as she hopped into a candy apple red convertible BMW and zoomed out of the parking lot, leaving me standing alone and feeling a little bewildered.

I climbed into my car and lit up a Black & Mild cigar, thinking about ol' blue-eyes asking me out for a so-called cup of coffee. She was up to something, but I sure as hell didn't know what.

Chapter 6

"WHAT IS HER NAME?" I wondered aloud as I cruised down the boulevard with my Black & Mild clinging to my bottom lip, still thinking about that morning's unexpected encounter with blue-eyes in the church parking lot. I smirked to myself, still amused to have captured the attention of a pale-skinned, blue-eyed chick with a killer body.

Never in my wildest dreams had I entertained the thought of dating a snowflake. But having not had the best luck with the sisters, maybe this change of pace would do me some good.

Most black women I'd dated turned out to be controlling,

gold diggers or both. It sounded cliché, but my track record offered plenty of proof that I needed to broaden my horizons.

At the very least, snowflakes were reputed to be beasts in the bedroom, so why rule out having a so-called cup of coffee with my newfound friend?

The local convenience store had my usual six pack of Coronas and a box of Black & Milds. Its owner, a dark-skinned Pakistani man, greeted me with his winning toothless smile.

"Attorney Banks," he said, walking from behind the counter as I approached with my purchases. As usual, he violently slapped me on the back of the neck. I wasn't sure if this was some custom of his or if he just hated Americans; either way, it hurt like hell.

Had it not been for his five-foot frame and the serious shortage of beer in the fridge at home, I'd have dropped him like a bad habit in about a half second.

"How was your day?" he demanded to know. Well now, my day stung.

He still beamed, squeezing my neck hard before finally releasing me.

Rubbing at the stinging pain, I managed to shoot him a half smile. "It was good."

"Did you arrest any criminals today?" he queried, his accent thick.

"No, I'm a lawyer, not a police officer," I reminded him for the hundredth time.

"Yes, that is right." He reached up and gripped the back of my neck again. "I remember now."

"How is your day?" Was it possible that my question would distract him enough to let go?

His face darkened and as I'd hoped, he dropped his hand from my neck.

But now, he looked aggrieved, blotchy in the face like a can of chopped ham, balling both hands into tight fists at his sides. Seething, he was. "Oh, my day, it is not good, Attorney Banks. No, no, my day is so, so bad. My daughter, you see, she is a slut!" he yelled, storming back behind the counter as I placed my cigars and beer next to the register and reached for my wallet.

Ha! Well, don't hold back! I thought. *Say what's really bothering you, why don't you?*

My stomach hurt from holding in pent-up laughter at his words.

"She is dating an American boy. I am very afraid she is what Americans call a whore."

He grabbed my items and scanned them with more force than necessary, slamming them down on the scanner, over and over.

Thank God it wasn't eggs today...

He made a habit of this brutality with my shopping, in fact, and I ought to have learned never to ask what was happening in his life, at least not until I had my groceries safely in a strong bag and was headed for the door. *Oh, not again,* I thought. *Why do I always wind him up?*

Now, I was hurriedly inserting my American Express gold card into the reader, willing it to process quickly. "Well, I'm saddened to hear that. I'm sure it will all get better."

"America is evil!" he shouted. "I hate this country."

With that, he threw my cigars into a plastic bag and shoved it toward me.

This old man had to be kidding. "So why the hell did you move to America?" I asked with an obvious attitude. This heathen needed a capitalist reality check. For one, he owned a profitable business on what he called 'foreign soil.' Two, he had repeat customers even though he could barely speak the language. And three, his profits came primarily from sales to Americans.

It would've been justified to slap the hell out of him right then and there, but I knew better.

Ungrateful maggot, I thought, yanking my card from the reader and jamming it back into my wallet. Swearing under my breath, I vowed never to return to this man's store.

Sadly, I'd be back as soon as my supply was low again.

"Why can't my daughter find a man like you?" the store owner suddenly blurted.

"Like me?" I repeated with a raised eyebrow.

I'd been born on the same American soil he seemed to despise.

"Yes, someone who will take care of her. Someone with good credit. Someone who will bow down to Allah."

"Bow down to Allah?" I shot back. "I was in church just this morning. So Allah will have to take a back seat."

"Young and dumb," he said, shaking his head. "Allahu Akbar the benevolent. You are the one true God. All praise due to Allah!" he shouted once, then again.

I didn't want to admit it, but his Allahu Akbar chant had just scared the hell out of me.

I needed to get my ass out of his establishment. "Well, have a great night." My voice was loud, interrupting him as he started into round three, then turning to head for the exit.

"You too, Attorney Banks," he shouted. "And make sure you arrest more bad guys tomorrow!"

"Will do!" I quickly tossed over my shoulder, shaking my head, pushing through the swinging doors and heading toward my car.

In the apartment twenty minutes later, I tossed my keys on the counter, kicked my shoes off and cracked open a Corona. *What a crazy day.* I lit up a Black & Mild. Today definitely warranted a beer and smoke session.

Two beers later, lounging on the couch and enjoying a slight buzz, I flipped on the TV to channel-surf, clicking through what felt like a million channels before stumbling onto 'New Jack City' playing on HBO. *Can't go wrong with some old-school Wesley Snipes.*

I tuned in, and before long, was sound asleep.

Chapter 7

IT HAD BEEN NEARLY three months since showing my face in the church, and it was clear my one-off visit hadn't done me any good. Blake had left me yet another threatening voice message reminding me that Sunday was reserved for the Lord.

If he didn't see me at church, I'd be on my way to an eternal fiery end. It would've made sense to be pissed at him, but after last night's blackout drinking and smoking binge, an old-fashioned, come-to-Jesus wake-up call might well be in order.

Dressed to the nines, I slid into my car, donned my Ray-Bans, and lit up a cigar before grabbing my phone. Backing out of my parking spot, one hand punched in Blake's number.

"Hello?" His voice sounded scratchy.

"What's up, Blake?" I exclaimed excitedly. "Ready for a morning of praise and worship?"

"What time is it, T.B.?" he yawned.

Déjà vu. "Please tell me you are not still in bed."

"Late night, bruh." He yawned a second time. "Why don't you go on to church? I'll stay here and catch up with my Saturday night sin since she's laying right here next to me."

"What happened to Sunday being the Lord's Day? And what about the lake of fire having many vacancies?"

"And I meant what I said. Sunday is the Lord's Day," he tossed back. "Maybe I don't show today, but God knows my heart. He's going to take some time gettin' to know yours but at least He's seen me a few times before. Now get to church, meet yourself a nice churchgoing woman and who knows, maybe next week, you'll be in my shoes."

"What?" I nearly choked on my cigar. "Your 'Saturday night sin' is from church?"

"Yes, sir," he whispered. "She leads the hospitality ministry and is also on the welcoming committee. Let's just say she welcomed me in with open arms and has proven very hospitable indeed. She mentioned I could come anytime. Every pun intended."

"Well, the lake of fire will have another two residents soon," I retorted, laughing despite my frustration.

"Don't be so quick to judge, TB. Despite my many short-comings, I am saved and sanctified by the blood of my Lord and Savior and have a one-way non-refundable ticket into Heaven for all eternity."

"So you keep telling me. Not sure where I'll be spending eternity, but since we're on the topic, I do have a question for you."

"Let's hear it."

"All right. You've said before that you follow Jesus. You call yourself a Christian, right? And you're trying to convince me, while your Saturday night conquest lies beside you, that no matter what you do, you're all set with God? Let's just say it doesn't really convey that wholesome, churchy vibe. Every weekend, you invite me out to church to learn about the same Jesus that my mother preached, but Jesus sure didn't protect her from my father.

"Can't say church has made much of a difference for you, either. So why should I bother?"

He laughed. "I got nothing but love for you, TB. And I know I'm not setting the best example. I'm not going to pretend that I have all of the answers, but I can assure you giving my life to Jesus was the best decision I ever made. The reason I invite you to church every week is because there is no love on earth greater than the perfect love of Christ. I know this already but you, bruh, still need to be sure of it. Accept it and it will change you. Now, get your ass in church and praise the Lord. Oh, and don't forget to say a prayer for me."

I sighed. "Sure, man."

"Peace, TB."

Moments later, I pulled into the church parking lot and popped a few Altoids again, just in case. I strolled through the double doors, hoping not to run into ol' blue-eyes.

After my last visit in which I'd completely blown her off, and after she'd been so direct the first time around, it was evident she'd call me out if we crossed paths again.

Unfortunately, as soon as I set foot inside the sanctuary, there she was.

This time, she was greeting an older black couple with that superficial smile. *Damn,* I thought, silently trying to creep past the three of them unnoticed.

"Brother Banks!" rang the voice of Mr. Chandler.

"Hey, Mr. Chandler," I muttered, trying to stay under the radar. "How the devil are you?"

The devil? What was I saying? "Sorry, it's just a saying. I…"

"Where have you been, son?" He ignored the faux pas and

threw his arm around my shoulder and squeezed tightly as if I was indeed his long-lost progeny coming home to pay a visit at last.

"Oh, me? I've just been working and staying out of trouble. You know how it is."

"Well, it's been too long. You do know that the only place to be on a Sunday morning is in the house of the Lord, don't you?" he questioned me.

"Yeah, I guess," I replied, edging my way toward the sanctuary doors while keeping my eyes on the blue-eyed demon still engrossed in conversation with the elderly couple.

I needed out of this conversation before she turned and pounced.

"What do you mean, 'you guess?'" quizzed Mr. Chandler, an eyebrow cocked. "Can you tell me another place you would rather be on a Sunday morning other than the house of the Lord?"

Before I could answer, my time was up. Though actually, I could think of a few places, if pressed. Did he really want me to have a go at listing them? No, probably not.

Sweat beads popped up on my brow as the blue-eyed woman turned, spotted me and beelined straight toward Mr. Chandler and me with something akin to a demonic, crazed look.

Anywhere but here, I silently begged, my heart pounding violently in my chest. *Please, Lord. Please, not here.* There was no excuse as to why I hadn't called.

Just lie! a voice inside my head suggested.

But deliberately lying in the house of the Lord seemed awfully wrong, especially for someone like me who'd come out today specifically seeking a new direction.

Tell her you lost her phone number, the voice prompted again. *The number was on a bit of paper, and it was in your pants pocket, and you washed your pants. In the machine. With bleach.*

That seemed a good idea until the thought came: sounds terrible to bleach a pair of pants.

A fierce battle was raging in my mind, and I was losing big time. *Or just tell her you are not interested in dating white girls! White girls are not sexy! I was headed downhill quickly.*

Blue-eyes had arrived in front of us; the jig was up.

"Greetings, Brother Chandler," she acknowledged politely. Then she turned a piercing stare my way. "Well, well, well! Brother Banks. It's been a long time."

"Yeah, I know. How are you?" I said in a nervous tone, pretending to be interested.

"Didn't I give you my phone number the last time you were

at church?" She cut right to the chase, glancing up at Mr. Chandler, who by this point was eyeing me like a hawk.

A pointy finger was jabbing into my sternum, making me edge backwards.

"Yeah, I meant to call you, but work's been so busy, and it'd be wrong to call and then not be able to give you my full attention. But I'll call you this week, okay?" Lie number one.

"Why don't you give me your phone number since you're so busy, Brother Banks? I will be sure to call you. Even when I'm busy, I'll always make time, like most people do."

"Well, you know I'm an old-fashioned man. I wouldn't feel right about having a woman call me first," I hedged, lying again, hoping it came across as chivalry. "It's not polite, you know?"

Lie number two because that was not the reason, far from it.

"Not polite? I'll tell you what's not polite. Sitting on a good woman's phone number and never calling!" she said, her lips downturned in an ugly grimace.

"I know. That's true, and I apologize. I'll make sure to call you tonight."

With lie number three, the bells of the church rang. *And the lies have it,* my inner voice told me, and I cringed, immediately regretting which voice had won the battle.

Everyone turned and headed into the sanctuary. Was that sick twisting feeling deep in my gut at all akin to that old Sunday school lesson about Peter denying Jesus three times?

Now in my seat, it was a relief to escape further conversation, and possible to feign deep prayer by clasping my hands together and shutting my eyes so tight they must've appeared glued.

Just before the sermon was over, the side door allowed me to sneak free, unwilling to chance yet another unpleasant rendezvous with that woman.

Safely in my car, my head leaned back against the headrest, my eyes closing again.

If this was the outcome of trying to turn over a new leaf, it had been a bad idea.

Chapter 8

BLAKE WAS LOUNGING at the bar, flirting with a female bartender when the most beautiful woman I had seen in months walked gracefully through the double doors of my favorite restaurant.

Who is she? She was certainly memorable, but no name came to me. As I finished off the last of my Corona and set it back on the restaurant's branded coaster, she strolled toward me.

Passing just a few feet away, she lowered herself onto a stool near the end of the bar where Blake was now blatantly reaching for the bartender's derriere.

Ouch, I thought, feeling the sting of her wordless rejection. I might as well be invisible.

"Are you trying to get us thrown out?" I growled in Blake's direction, keeping my eyes on the mystery woman.

"She wants me," Blake shouted, loud enough for everyone in the restaurant to hear. "They all want me!" He laughed maniacally.

"Yeah, yeah, yeah." I rolled my eyes. "You're God's gift to women, playboy!"

As I was contemplating the best opening line to break the ice with my mystery woman, a tall, sharply dressed gentleman with a distinguished salt-and-pepper beard roamed past.

He moved straight toward my dream woman, rested his hand on her shoulder and leaned in to greet her as she turned and beamed up at him.

Her smile lit up her whole face, making her even more captivating.

Damn, I thought, flagging down the bartender. "Can I get another Corona and a shot of Hennessy?" Just when it seemed I'd found London's replacement, this Terrell Owens look-alike had to show up. Out of the corner of my eye, I watched the two of them embracing tightly.

It didn't help that his hands were moving all over her hips and down to grip that fine ass I'd been appreciating only moments ago. Seconds later, my voyeurism abruptly ended, startled by the restaurant pager on the bar buzzing violently, vibrating its way along the counter.

Saved by the bell. I didn't need to see any more of that particular scene.

Otherwise, it would end up playing on repeat in my head later. My shot went down in one, the Corona following. "Yo, Blake?"

"What's up, TB?"

"Time to go." The flashing buzzer clutched in my grasp was indicating our table was ready.

"Give me a few minutes, TB. I'm trying to convince my new friend to let me take her out on a date." He grinned and winked at the bartender.

I sighed. "Whatever, man."

My voice and tone were those of a hater, but despite not wanting to admit it, I was hating; wasn't it true that fate was constantly working against me? We'd been wingmen for each other for a long time, but lately, it had seemed like he got all of the women and all I ever got was let down. Not that I believed in fairy tales or anything, but it felt as if my beautiful princess would never come. I sighed again, following the hostess to the table.

"Your server will be right with you." She smiled, handing me a menu.

My new vantage point offered a great position from which to survey the room.

Happy hour was wrapping up, but the restaurant was still jam-packed with a wide mix of patrons ranging from corporate bigwigs to leather-vested motorcyclists. A gang of women a few tables over sat openly eyeballing me.

As I made eye contact, a heavy woman with bright pink hair—who I assumed was the leader of the pack—rose from her seat, sauntering my way with her drink in hand, licking her lips as if I was dessert after her meal. I sighed, knowing this type, bracing for the worst.

"Hi," she said as she slid a chair from under my table and took a seat, uninvited.

My eyes scanned the bar for Blake to save me, but he was now behind it with his sleeves rolled up, serving drinks. "So much for my wingman," I grumbled to myself.

My unwanted guest removed the straw from her drink and slowly circled it with her tongue, sensual and provocative. Only it wouldn't work, not on me and not right now.

"What's your name?" she purred.

"Um, Todd."

"What is such a handsome man like you doing sitting here all alone?" she pressed.

"I'm waiting on someone." I peered toward the bar a second time and spotted Blake grinning at me like an idiot with his thumbs up.

"Get it, TB, get it!" he shouted.

"Get what?" I mouthed, glaring at him.

He leaped over the bar, jogging toward the table.

"Hey, beautiful." He smiled at the pink-haired seductress. "My name's Blake, and this is my boy, TB."

"Hey," she said, signaling for one of her girls. "I'm Darla, but my friends call me Pinky."

"Pinky," I replied. "Because of your hair?"

"Yessss." She nodded. "Handsome and smart. I like that."

"Did my boy tell you he was single?" Blake prompted unnecessarily.

"Oh, um, I'm not really single," I lied, glaring at him. "I have my eyes on someone special."

"Oh yeah, TB? And who might that be?"

"You know," I said, trying to laugh it off. "Stop playing."

"Seriously, what's her name again?"

"London," I said with an attitude. "Her name is London."

The women raised their eyes to heaven in a collective eye roll, not even making an attempt to conceal it. It conveyed something like *that's a stupid name, and pretentious.*

"Pinky, let's go," said her counterpart. "These losers don't know real women when they see one."

Pinky grabbed her drink from the table and stood.

Dropping a scathing scowl on me, she announced, "You couldn't handle all of these curves anyway." She turned on her heel and stormed after her friend.

"Yeah, TB." Blake laughed aloud. "She has curves for decades."

I didn't respond. *What kind of man can handle 300 pounds of ass anyway?* I thought viciously, watching Pinky and her friend take their seats. Pinky immediately leaned in and began speaking and gesturing animatedly to her girls, hiding her mouth behind her hand.

It won't be anything worth hearing anyway, so she needn't bother.

Blake earned himself an intense, menacing stare. He quickly took a step backwards, raising his hands in front of him. "What? I was trying to hook you up, TB!"

"Yeah, well, the next time you want to hook me up, please make sure they don't weigh 200 pounds more than I do."

"So you're not into BBWs, huh?" The corner of Blake's mouth twitched upward.

"What the hell are BBWs?" This change of topic was irritating.

"Big Black Women!" He laughed loudly and jabbed me in the arm before darting back to the bar. I tried to refocus on the menu. That, too, had nothing to offer me.

Setting it back on the table, my eyes caught the hostess walking by to seat a couple at the table next to me. Gray-beard and his stunning girl were now just a few feet away.

With her green eyes, long silky hair and toned body, there was no way I could ignore her. But with gray-beard around, there was no room to make a move either.

I was going to need about six more drinks to even make it to dessert.

As he pulled out her chair and helped her to sit, I tried to play it cool, keeping my head straight and just glancing at her out of the corner of my eye. But as he took his seat, I caught gray-beard's eyes just as they were catching me! Staring me down, he raised his fist as if part of the Black Panther party. Busted, I thought, nodding my head to acknowledge his fist gesture.

He returned my nod with a wide Colgate smile.

Returning his attention to his date, he reached over with one hand to entwine his fingers with hers, then cupped her face with his other hand as he leaned close to whisper something in her ear.

I tried not to watch, but couldn't shove down the envy coursing through me. Why couldn't that be me? London came back to mind, but this thought only made me feel more alone.

"Hi there. Are you ready to place your order?" a freckle-faced waitress chirped suddenly, catching me off guard.

"Um…" I quickly glanced over the menu, but the only thing I had an appetite for was the unavailable woman sitting opposite. "Give me a few more minutes."

She grinned. "Take your time." She turned and walked away, but just a few seconds later, she returned. Still not ready, thanks must have shown on my face, but before the words escaped, she bent down to ear level and whispered, "She's not the only beautiful woman in here tonight."

"Huh? What do you mean?" I played dumb, knowing full well who she was talking about.

"You're a very handsome guy." She flashed an appreciative smile at me. "But trying to eat from another's table seems a little pathetic, don't you think?"

"I was just admiring the view." The comment was trying to cover my embarrassment.

She straightened up. "Oh, so that's what they're calling it nowadays, huh?"

Unsure how to respond, I forced a laugh. "Good one."

"Look, I've been waitressing here for years and I've seen plenty of people come and go. I'm not the rain-on-your-parade kind of girl and it's not really any of my business, but have you thought about just waiting on God?"

I glanced up at her in surprise. "Waiting on God for what?"

Chapter 9

THE FOLLOWING MORNING, I was slightly hung over from the night out with Blake and running late for my 9:00 a.m. with Madison Perry, the therapist who, in just three short sessions, already knew more about me than my birth mother. My tires screeched into the parking lot, and I dashed inside the office with seconds to spare.

"Good morning," a cute, brown-eyed receptionist greeted me. "May I help you?"

"Good morning." I smiled. "My name is Todd Banks and I have a 9:00 a.m. appointment with Madison Perry."

"Do you have your insurance card, Mr. Banks?" She peered

up at me from her seat behind the desk. I removed the plastic card from my wallet and handed it to her.

"Thank you." She scanned the card and handed it back. "Please take a seat and I'll let Dr. Perry know you're here."

I headed over to the waiting area and took a seat next to an elderly gentleman sporting a Tom Brady jersey.

"Good morning," he greeted me.

"Morning." I grabbed a Sports Illustrated magazine from the table in front of me and flipped through the pages to pass the time. After a few moments, out walked Madison Perry.

"Todd," she said, extending her hand.

"Good morning, Dr. Perry." We shook hands and her skin was soft.

"Follow me," she said, turning down a short hallway.

She led me into her office and indicated a black leather couch in the corner of the room. I sat down, resting my elbows on my knees as I watched her get settled in the chair opposite me. Dr. Perry was drop-dead gorgeous. Her long blonde hair, hazel eyes and petite athletic frame were stunning, and she was impeccably dressed to match.

Therapy was still new to me—these three recent visits were all I had to go on—but I was pretty sure Dr. Perry wasn't your average therapist.

"So, Todd," she asked, picking up a black padfolio and silver Cross pen. "How have you been since our last meeting?"

"It's been interesting," I began. "That's the only word that comes to mind." I swung my legs onto the end of the couch—though it seemed rude to do so, but I did it anyway to get more comfortable—resting my arms behind my head. Now, I was pretty much lying down, eyes closing, reminiscing. "You don't mind me taking full advantage of your cozy couch, do you?"

She laughed.

It sounded slightly taken aback but she answered, "If that's what gets you to talk, go for it."

"Yes, well, I met an amazing woman on the train, and went back to that church we talked about before."

"Tell me about the woman from the train. I take it you spoke to her? What's her name?"

"Well." I sat up again and leaned forward. "Her name's London, and she's the most beautiful woman I have ever met. I believe she's the one for me, doc."

"The one?" She searched my eyes. "What makes you think she's the one?"

"Because she's captivating and intriguing and unlike any woman I have ever met." I lay back on the couch again. "I just wish I could find her." Those words were mouthed softly to myself, but just my luck, Dr. Perry heard me. It seemed she was attuned to hearing everything sometimes, even the words that stayed unspoken. Maybe she was more of a psychiatrist than a regular therapist; in either event, it felt as though she was always 'hearing' things the client didn't even say. Her eyes were in constant evaluation mode, and she cocked her head as if it helped her to listen and digest the information at some deeper level.

"Wait a minute." She closed the padfolio and stared at me. "Just a moment ago, you said you believe she is the one. But did I hear you correctly that you don't even know where she is?"

"It's a long story, doc," I said, evading. "Can we talk about something else?"

"Sure." She reopened her padfolio and jotted down a few notes. "Tell me about the church you've been attending. Does it help you?"

Help me? God only knows the answer to that.

"It's a great church with a lot of nice people," I said.

"Great." She nodded. "It's important to feel connected with a community. How did you find this church… how did you come across it in the first place?"

"My friend Blake invited me."

"Excellent. And will you be going again this weekend?"

"Um, don't think so."

"Why is that? If it makes you feel connected…"

Those were your words, not mine.

"Well, there's this woman there and she's pretty pushy. But I don't want to talk about that."

Hell. The poor woman must have been running dry of topics since there were so many no-go zones. "I'm sorry," tripped from my tongue. "You must think this is an awkward conversation."

"A little, but all right. There is never any productive reason to force a client to discuss uncomfortable things. These subjects we can cover another time, when it works better for you and feels natural, all right? So, how is work going then?"

There was a pause as a deep exhale left my lungs.

"Can we talk about that?" she probed. "Tell me if it's uncomfortable."

"It's fine, it's fine. Just thinking is all. Call it a lawyer habit. The answers don't always come fast. But I love my job." I turned my head to meet her eyes. "My great paralegal keeps things straight for me and I'm winning my cases regularly. What is there not to like?"

"I'm glad you feel positively about the value and impact of your professional endeavors. It's more important than people often realize. Many times, that's where we get our greatest sense of self-belief and value." She uncrossed her legs, recrossing them the opposite way.

A shiver ran down my spine and I looked away.

"How is your social life?" she continued. "What have you been doing outside of work lately? You are taking time out, I trust, like we discussed last time?"

I rolled my eyes. This was the reason I'd started coming to therapy in the first place. "God forbid. I'm so tired of dating crazy women, doc," I huffed, suddenly irritated. Why did her question irk me so much? But on the tip of my tongue was *I don't want to talk about that.*

At the same time, my brain whirred, you can't. *You can't keep shutting her down like this.*

She knew what she was doing, so I made a mature decision, went ahead and let it out. "It seems like every woman out there is insecure, controlling and bossy!"

"Based on your testimony about London earlier, not all women fall into that category, Todd," she said, eyeing me carefully. "Perhaps they're not entirely the problem. Perhaps you are simply choosing the wrong types of women. Or perhaps the problem lies partly in yourself."

"What do you mean?" I sat upright and stared directly at her.

She closed the padfolio and carefully placed it on top of the small wooden table beside her.

"Let's cut to the chase, Todd." She leaned forward, interlacing her fingers and cupping her knee with them. "From what you've shared in our time together so far, I suspect the reason you're finding yourself with bossy, controlling women is because you don't believe you deserve better. You constantly second-guess yourself and rely on the opinions of others."

"What?"

"Case in point."

"I don't understand." I felt more confused now than before I'd walked into her office.

"Think about it. You've just told me that every relationship you've had has been with someone who displays the three characteristics you claim to be sick and tired of: insecurity, bossiness, and control issues," she continued. "Clearly, your choices are consistent. But when we are not happy with where we wind up, we have to ask ourselves: what brought me here?

"Or rather, why did I bring myself here? If it keeps on happening and grows into a pattern, then the question has to become, why do I keep bringing myself back to this place, time and again? You see, you are the common denominator. You are the one who makes the choices.

"And these are conscious choices, Todd. We each decide with whom we will enter into a romantic relationship. Because of your own insecurities, you choose women who have been abused in other relationships and they long for a knight in shining armor to rescue them from their past and from themselves. Their neediness makes you feel needed, at least initially.

"And again, if I'm perfectly blunt, which as your therapist I need to be, then you also must consider why you have this great rush to identify someone as your next partner. You have barely seen this 'London' lady, and you don't know where she lives. She didn't give you her number and yet here you are, saying *she's the one*. And I'll wager you thought that about the others too.

"Things will keep going sour if you persist in rushing in blindly."

Ouch. That hurt.

I thought back over my past few flings. It was impossible to think of a single exception. "True," I begrudgingly admitted. "All that you say is true. I don't know why I do it either."

"I have already told you why you do it. Can you remember what I suggested it was?"

"Insecurity."

"Exactly. And weeks or months into your relationships, as the initial infatuation fades, these women begin to reveal themselves because let's be frank, you entered into a degree of intimacy without knowing anything much about them. You have insecurities so you're attracted to women who make you feel you can help them in some way. You like the woman to be needy of you.

"But at the same time, it's a big ask, Todd, to ask for a woman who is needy and insecure but who won't become controlling and possessive because these traits go hand in hand. You cannot keep blaming the women for that: I reiterate, you chose them because of these allied factors.

"In time, and no doubt as you become more confident in your position in the relationship, their insecurities resurface, and they become bossy and aggressive. They start to demand all of your time, want to know your every move and become angry when you want something for yourself. Before long, you find yourself in the same place you started, searching for a way out.

"There is only one way to avoid this. It's to make yourself feel secure outside of a relationship, then look for women with a secure attachment style. Someone more stable."

I'd lived through this exact relationship pattern enough times to know she was right.

"You sure know the type," I observed with chagrin.

"Todd." She leaned in closer. "This is no bad dream. This is your life we are talking about. If you want something different, you have to make a change. I can help you to effect the change but first, it's up to you to commit to making it. There's no rush. Please think about this for as long as you require and come back to me at any future point."

"That's why I'm here, doc," I replied, frustrated. "If it's so obvious, then tell me what to do." I folded my arms across my chest. My plea sounded so plaintive. If she hadn't said all that she had, I would never have faced up to this. She'd been honest and frank. It hurt but I needed it.

"Haven't you heard a word of what I've been saying to you, Todd?"

Now, I was hurting again. What did she want from me?

Hadn't I just said she should tell me the way out of all this misery, out of my struggle?

Why wasn't that the right answer?

She searched my eyes. "I'm not here to tell you what to do. I'm here to help you realize on your own what you need to do. You need to contemplate it and commit to wanting a change."

"Yeah, I have been listening, but… And I do want to change but…"

"You're asking me for a way out, but the door has always been open. You can choose to walk out any time you want. You only need to make a different choice." Glancing at the clock, she rose from her seat. "Our time today is up. See you again next week?"

"Yeah, same time."

I felt deflated, worse than on walking in.

It felt akin to one of those terrible arguments in a relationship, the ones in which we'd go around and around on the same subject for hours, only leaving me more confused but at the same time, processing how, yet again, I was the one at fault.

Chapter 10

A FEW WEEKS LATER, I woke up on a sunny Sunday morning. It was time to give the church another chance. Perhaps I'd been wrong about the people there. They'd been pretty welcoming, especially ol' blue-eyes and with all the therapy lately, I was feeling confident.

By now, I'd figured out how to handle myself.

I cruised over to the church, not bothering to call Blake this time, and pulled into a parking spot. Making my way into the building, I was greeted by blue-eyes herself. She was as beautiful as ever. On a whim, I decided to give her my number. What did I have to lose?

"Thank you, Todd." Her voice rang with excitement. "I'll call you after church today to set up that coffee date."

"Today?" My tone was nervous. "You're not wasting any time, are you?"

"Not wasting time? You're kidding, right? May I remind you it's been over five months since we met, Todd." She removed her cell phone from her purse and added my number to her contacts. "Oh, and I'll need a picture of you."

"For what?"

"So when you call, I'll know it's you."

"Shouldn't my name be enough to know who I am?"

"I'm a visual kind of girl." She winked, holding up her phone and tapping the screen to focus it. "Say cheese!"

Before I could say anything, she had snapped the picture.

Mr. Chandler was standing there in the background, staring at us with what looked like a measure of suspicion in his eyes. Stepping forward, he grabbed me by the back of the arm.

"Excuse me, sister. Give me a minute to educate Brother Banks on how we treat women in the church," he said.

"Take your time, Brother Chandler," she allowed.

"Listen, son," he began. He had me cornered. "I don't know what you're up to, but the women in our church are all pure before God. Pure they enter here, and pure they remain."

"Pure before God?" It echoed Blake's description of his bedmate several weeks earlier. "Can you tell me where to find someone from the hospitality ministry or welcome committee?"

"Sister Jacobs," he resounded, his voice echoing through the lobby. His hand still gripped the back of my arm firmly as he steered me back across the room.

"Yes, Brother Chandler," blue-eyes replied, smiling at me.

"Where can we find Sister Goode?"

"She called the church about an hour ago saying that she wasn't feeling well. Unfortunately, she will not be here today." She glanced down, still with my picture pulled up on her phone. "Is there anything I can help with?"

"No, thank you," Mr. Chandler replied, finally loosening his grip on my arm. "Brother Banks wanted to meet with her."

"About what?"

"Oh, um, I was thinking about joining the church today and wanted to know more about what ministry might be open to me."

Their faces transformed before my eyes, hope blossoming across their features. Regret dawned in me the very moment the words slipped out of my mouth.

"Praise the Lord." Mr. Chandler's eyes began to water. "This is the best decision you could ever have made, son." His voice rang with sincerity, multiplying my guilt.

What have I done? my inner voice rang out desperately, racking my brain for a way out of this unholy mess. "I'm still thinking about it," I backpedaled. "Nothing's set in stone, Mr. Chandler."

With my attention on Mr. Chandler, Sister Jacobs almost bowled me over, launching herself toward me and pressing her body against mine.

"You will love it here," she whispered fervently, staring deep into my eyes. I grabbed her shoulders and moved her to arms' length before she got a rise out of me.

"Thanks." My tone was short. "Still not sure, though."

Despite my attempts to undo the damage and distance myself from the situation, my proclamation spread quickly. In what seemed like a matter of moments, the whole congregation had heard the glad tidings and everyone within shouting distance began congratulating me.

I needed to escape this lunacy before it got seriously out of control. But before any move was possible, Pastor Patterson appeared in the sanctuary doors, spotted me, and headed my way.

Damn. She strode toward me.

In a last-ditch attempt, my whole body pivoted to make its escape, but Mr. Chandler blocked me, smiling brightly as he shared the news with several nearby parishioners.

"Praise the Lord!" came loud and clear from several people.

I pivoted back around, finding myself face-to-face with Pastor Patterson. Sweat dotted my forehead as she extended her hand and smiled.

"Welcome home." She greeted me like a prodigal son as we shook hands, her soft fingers grabbing for mine. "I hear you are joining the church today. Is that right?"

Her look was piercing and damn near hypnotic.

Don't look her in the eyes. But my body was responding to her stunning looks.

"I'm still thinking about it." A crooked smile anointed my face. "Though the fellowship here is wonderful and heartwarming."

"Well, we would love to have you as part of our family." She flashed her pearly whites, somehow doubling her allure. My heart was beating violently against my chest as she stepped closer, a light perfume washing over me. "And I will work with you personally to make sure you feel comfortable here," she added in a low tone.

My defenses had completely crumbled.

My conversation with Blake about meeting a nice woman in church, someone I could sleep with, bounced around my skull. "Um, yeah, I really like this church."

With another smile, Pastor Patterson stepped forward again and embraced me. Swept up by the moment and her sweet scent, I latched onto her, breathing her in and pressing my body against hers with the intimacy of lovers. I opened my eyes, searched her face and wet my lips.

Completely forgetting where we were, I was ready to go in for what I was certain would be the kiss of a lifetime. Before I made a fool of myself, Mr. Chandler yanked me by the shoulder and spun me away.

"I look forward to working with you, Brother Banks," Pastor Patterson called. My eyes followed her as she stepped back inside the inner sanctuary, followed by two well-muscled men.

"Boy, are you crazy?" Mr. Chandler seemed to scold me.

"Crazy?" I was confused.

"You were nearly molesting Pastor Patterson, boy," he said, shaking my shoulder and rebuking me as he might a child. "You are lucky her bodyguards didn't break your damn neck for that outrageous display of harassment." He released my shoulder and glared.

"She didn't seem to have a problem with my church hug," I defended.

Before Mr. Chandler could reply, Pastor Patterson was suddenly back at our sides.

"I meant what I said, Brother Banks," she stated, handing me her business card. "Call me if you need anything."

Slipping her card into my pocket, I smiled knowingly at Mr. Chandler.

"Thank you, Pastor Patterson."

"We have a wonderful seat in the front for you today."

She reached for my hand and escorted me to a seat right up front, in the very first pew. It appeared I was among several prominent church leaders. "Take very good care of our special guest," she instructed an older couple seated to my right.

The sanctuary slowly filled as parishioners trickled in from the lobby. I glanced around, wondering if this special treatment was customary for soon-to-be church members, but didn't ask. Either way, I was sure looking forward to getting to know Pastor Patterson outside of church. I settled into my seat, my mind drifting as the service began.

Several hymns and a surprisingly short sermon later, an associate pastor announced the open altar call, inviting guests to give their lives to God and join the church. With Pastor Patterson's card already in my pocket, I remained seated. Now that I'd connected with her, what was the point of joining the church? Anything I wanted to know about God I could learn firsthand from her. Following a few church announcements and a final hymn, the service finally ended.

I stood up, stretched and headed for the exit.

"See you next week, Todd!" Pastor Patterson waved as she shook hands and chatted with several church members clustered around her.

Waving back, I reached into my pocket and fingered her card as though holding the winning lottery ticket. *Jackpot!* I smiled to myself and made my way out to my car.

A Black & Mild was just nestling in my fingers when ol' blue-eyes appeared at my window.

"Hey, Brother Banks." She stared me down. Cutting straight to the point, she asked, "Why didn't you join the church today like you promised you would?"

"I didn't feel the Holy Spirit was leading me to join just yet." That almost sounded believable, I laughed to myself, slipping my key into the ignition.

"Hmm. Well, when are we going to have that cup of coffee?" she pressed.

Damn, she's insistent. Should have never handed over my number!

How to respond to that? "I'm going to be busy all week with court."

"How about tomorrow during lunch?"

"Lunch may work, but…"

"So lunch it is," she concluded, skipping over the start of my excuse. "I'll text you the address."

"I'll look at my calendar and get back to you later tonight."

She rolled her eyes and smiled. "Brother Banks, do you even know my name?"

Mr. Chandler had been referring to her as Sister Jacobs earlier. "Yes," I said proudly. "It's Sister Jacobs, right?"

"My first name, Todd?"

"Oh, um, hmmm…"

"It's Sarah." She leaned inside my car and planted a soft kiss to my frontal lobe. "I'm so happy you agreed to meeting tomorrow. I have been looking forward to getting to know you since you first set foot in church."

Despite my disinterest, my ego puffed at her implied compliment. "Oh? Why's that?"

"You will see." She smiled mischievously. "See you tomorrow, honey."

Chapter 11

LOOKING AND SMELLING like a million dollars, I strode confidently into Legal Seafood at noon on the dot. I was rocking a custom-made gray two-piece Ralph Lauren suit, a sharp white button-down with French cuffs and a pair of cognac-colored wingtip shoes. To make a good impression, I'd even asked my admin, Judy, to call ahead for reservations.

To say I was putting my best foot forward with Sarah was an understatement.

Admittedly, her parting comment and devious smile from yesterday had me curious. I wasn't sure what she had up her sleeve, but was ready to find out.

"Hello, Mr. Banks," the hostess greeted me warmly. I'd considered it a good omen that the address Sarah had texted me was to a restaurant I frequented regularly.

"Hey, Alyssa. I have a reservation for two today."

"For two?" she questioned, raising her eyebrows.

"Her name is Sarah."

"She must be a very special woman, Mr. Banks. Follow me," she said, leading me to a prime table on the outer balcony. "Your server will be with you momentarily."

"Thanks."

I took my seat and picked up the menu. Skimming through to see if they'd added anything new, a well-dressed gentleman a couple tables over asked his lunch companion, "Who is she?"

"I don't know," his tablemate enthused. "But I would pay good money to find out."

I looked up, curious about the source of their comments, quickly scanning. My jaw dropped. Sauntering toward me was a stunningly gorgeous dark-haired woman rocking a pair of close-fitting jeans, a stylish gray and black pinstripe shirt with the sleeves neatly rolled up, and black high-heeled sandals buckled around her ankles. As she walked, her eyes took in the room.

She smiled at those who made eye contact, finally stopping at my table.

"Hi, Todd." She smiled down at me seductively.

Quickly gathering my wits, I rose from my seat to greet her. "Hey, Sarah!" Every other man in the joint was now my enemy. It was time to stake my claim before someone else did.

"I'm sorry I'm late," she beseeched, stepping forward to wrap her arms around my neck as her eyes held mine. I gladly returned her embrace. For the first time since agreeing to meet with her, it just didn't matter that I was out with a woman of a different race.

Her beauty was entrancing.

"You look great," she complimented me.

"So do you." I was forcing myself to hold her gaze instead of devouring her accentuated curves. I pulled her seat out from under the table. "Please join me."

"Thank you."

While her looks alone would have made Sarah a prize even if she'd been completely incapable of intelligent conversation, I soon found myself genuinely enjoying her company.

An hour later, full and satisfied, my inner voice proclaimed how I'd misjudged her. She was more laid-back than I'd expected, and I could see myself hanging out with her again.

As we stepped into the elevator to head back to the parking lot, she turned. "I had a great time, Todd." She grabbed my hands, reeling me closer. "Can we do this again?"

Despite my appreciation for her looks and her company, still I paused, my heart smacking against my ribs. It would be so easy to say yes, but did I really want things to escalate with her?

What about London, the girl who still wandered through my mind daily? What about Pastor Patterson and her promises of one-on-one instruction? *What do you really want, Todd?*

Like the therapist said, you need to make your choice! No one else can make it for you!

The pressure of the moment intensified. Perplexed and frustrated at my own indecision, the easiest answer seemed to be the solution. "Sure. I would like that."

"Awesome." She smiled, squeezing my fingers as we exited the elevator. Reaching her car, I opened the door for her to get in. When she was safely buckled in her seatbelt, I smiled at her, then turned to find my own ride. Seconds later, she called out to me.

"Todd, wait!"

Spinning back around, she was suddenly face-to-face with me. Before I could say a word, she reached up, grabbed the back of my head and kissed me hard.

"What was that for?" I looked down at her, trying to calm the surge of butterflies in my stomach.

"You're an amazing man, Todd," she murmured, slipping her right hand into mine, raising the left to cup the side of my face. "I think I'm falling in love with you."

Quickly searching her eyes for some trace of humor, there was only passion in her gaze. Surely it was too soon for such a confession? Some distance between us was needed, pronto.

Plus, what exactly had she seen in me that was 'amazing'? I wasn't fond of hyperbole.

"Listen." My fingers grasped Sarah's wrist to pry her hand from my face, also extricating my other hand from her grip. "You're an amazing woman and I had a great time hanging out with you today, but I'm really not looking to be in a relationship with anyone just now."

Her face fell. "But why?" she pleaded, tears in her eyes. "Is it because I'm white and you're black? I don't care about that. What does color have to do with love? Look me in the eyes and tell me you didn't enjoy our first kiss. Kisses do not lie, Todd!"

She was right; I couldn't deny the surge of attraction in our kiss. Still, I didn't feel confident a relationship was what I needed, especially an interracial one; the race card was a major factor.

Sure, we'd had a wonderful time today, but what would my mother think if I brought home a white woman? I bit my lip, trying to find my approach.

As I hesitated, her tears overflowed, slowly tracking down her face.

"Well, we can be friends," I ventured. "But…"

"But what, Todd?" she asked, pinning me with her eyes.

She clutched the back of my neck and dragged me forward, locking her lips with mine a second time. As she pressed her body against me, our tongues danced in perfect unison and again the heat was rising, despite my unwillingness to commit. If circumstances had permitted, I would have taken her back to my office for a midday rendezvous.

As the kiss escalated, she sighed and let out a faint moan. "I do love you, Todd."

"Whoa." I quickly stepped back, the mood broken. "I'm not ready to be in an exclusive relationship with anyone. And how can you love someone you just met?"

"But you are my soulmate," she professed, still crying.

"Have you lost your damn mind? You don't even know me. And I'm not in love with you or anyone else." I turned and beelined for my car, refusing to look back.

"Wrong!" she shouted after me. "You are in love with Pastor Patterson! I saw how you looked at her," she accused. Behind me, her car door slammed, followed by the screech of tires.

Slipping into my car, I threw my vehicle into reverse and headed back to my office, nearly shaking with disbelief. Had that really just happened? She was a crazy one, no doubt.

I should have trusted my instincts and never agreed to have lunch with her.

It went back to what my therapist had said. I rushed in, always with needy women, and reaped the payback for that. Here it was again. As always, *mea culpa*.

Chapter 12

"SO, HOW WAS your lunch date?" Judy questioned without looking up as I opened my office door.

"A complete disaster."

"What happened?"

"Did I get any calls while I was out?"

"Yes." She smiled. "Pastor Patterson called!"

I spun on my heels expectantly. "What did she want?"

"She didn't say. Just asked that you call her when you can, Mr. Banks." She handed me a pink sticky note with Pastor Patterson's name and number on it.

Seizing the note, I darted into my office, closed the door, and picked up the phone. I punched in the number, then waited impatiently, my knee bouncing under my desk. After five rings, I got her voicemail. "Please leave a message at the beep."

"Hi, it's Todd. My admin told me you called earlier. Please phone me back at your earliest convenience." I left my direct number, then hung up. Wishing I'd been able to speak with her, I sighed, then stood and reopened my office door.

I found Judy standing on the other side, looking concerned.

"Are you sure everything is okay?" she asked.

"Fine," I replied curtly.

"All right," she accepted. "You have a visitor," she added. "Sarah Jacobs is here to see you."

"What?"

"I told her to wait in the lobby…"

"Tell her that I've left the office for the day."

"I would, but…"

"But what?"

"She told me she wasn't waiting. She'll be up any moment."

The words had barely made it out of her mouth when Sarah turned the corner, coming speed-walking toward me as if on some kind of a mission.

"Should I call security?" Judy asked with concern.

"No," I said, feeling as if starring in a scene from *Fatal Attraction*.

"Can we talk?" Sarah pushed past me into my office and sat down.

"Are you sure you don't want me to call security?" Judy whispered, staring at Sarah.

"I'm good. Thanks, Judy."

I ventured back into my office and seated myself behind my desk, trying to figure out a way to get Sarah out of my office. As soon as I sat down, the phone rang. "Yes, Judy."

"Mr. Banks, Pastor Patterson is here to see you. She is waiting in the lobby."

What is Pastor Patterson doing here? My hands were gripping the phone tightly as I peered over the desk at Sarah, who stared back at me with lust-filled eyes.

I quickly prioritized my newly announced visitor over the one sitting before me. "Thank you, Judy," I replied. "I'll be right out." I hung up the phone and snapped my laptop shut, giving up on work for the day. I'd had enough of women showing up to my office uninvited.

"Do you have to go?" Sarah leaned over the desk, reaching for my hand.

I leaned back, evading her grasp and made a show of stuffing my laptop and a stack of case files into my backpack. "Not yet, but you do," I told her. "An urgent matter's come up that I need to handle right away."

"We really need to talk, Todd," she reminded, sounding bothered. I ignored her. It irked the hell out of me that she had shown up here like a woman obsessed.

Then, she expected me to drop everything and talk? It simply wasn't going to happen.

"I don't need to talk, and especially not at work. Never at work."

"Then where?" Her voice was high-pitched, almost edging toward tearful again. This was all a bit much, wasn't it? This woman barely knew me! What would she be like if we got involved?

Standing abruptly, I walked to the door, indicating she should exit before me, then quickly walked her down the short hallway to the elevator. My finger jabbed at the 'down' button, every sinew of my body anxious for the elevator's familiar 'ding,' hoping she wasn't going to try to reopen our conversation in the middle of the corridor.

When the elevator doors finally slid open, I turned.

"Enjoy the rest of your day, Ms. Jacobs."

She stepped inside but turned to face me. "Ms. Jacobs? You'd only call me Ms. Jacobs if you're being nasty to me."

Isn't that a line from a Janet Jackson song?

It distracted me enough to let me be caught off guard when she stepped back out of the elevator, throwing her arms around my neck and licking the side of my face.

"Are you crazy?" I wiped my face with the sleeve of my suit coat, glancing around to be sure no one had seen her antics.

She flashed a wicked smile and slowly stepped back inside of the elevator. "I'll call you tonight." She winked as the doors closed.

Apparently, she hadn't heard a word.

Suddenly, she was reminding me of Jodi Arias, the girl who'd stalked and stabbed her suitor to death; that whole criminal trial from Court TV came back.

Stay away from all those needy ones, my inner voice said.

But the whole question was how?

Chapter 13

FRUSTRATED AND IRRITATED, I headed back toward Judy's desk, ready to invite Pastor Patterson up to the office. It was so exhausting that people were breaking my please do not show up uninvited rule; the sooner this impromptu meeting was over with, the better.

Around the corner, Judy was there, heavily engaged in fashion and makeup talk with Pastor Patterson, seated comfortably in front of her.

Apparently, no waiting in the lobby these days, I thought, managing not to roll my eyes.

"Pastor Patterson." I greeted her with a forced smile. "What an unexpected surprise." Like Sarah, Pastor Patterson was dressed to impress. Rocking a fitted knee-length black skirt, a crisp white button-down and black high heel pumps, her whole ensemble accentuated flawless curves. Her makeup was immaculate, and her beautiful long hair hung neatly in a ponytail.

Her look was a far cry from the long, pastoral robes she wore at church.

"Attorney Banks!" She stood and reached out her hand. "I was in the neighborhood and thought I would swing by to discuss the ministry with you."

Despite my irritation at her unannounced visit, her beauty was captivating.

I still didn't like surprise visitors, but if they looked this good and weren't crazy like Sarah, perhaps I could make an exception.

"Judy?" I planted my hands firmly on her desk.

"Yes, Mr. Banks."

"Please let any callers know I will be out of the office for the remainder of the day."

"What about your 4:00 p.m. meeting with Mr. Gammon?"

"Reschedule it for first thing tomorrow."

"I'm on it."

Smiling broadly, I ushered Pastor Patterson into my office,

appreciating the view as she preceded me. I watched as her eyes scanned the room, taking in the decor.

Slowly, she strolled around the office, admiring my degree certificates, awards, and accomplishments. I waited patiently, noticing where her attention was drawn. "You are a well-rounded individual, aren't you?" she stated, running her fingers over the silver-plated Cross pen lying on my desk as she finished her rounds and turned to face me.

"Not really," I said humbly. "Just an ordinary man with a job."

"Oh, no," she said, stepping forward and leaning in. "You are much more than ordinary."

My heart rate kicked up involuntarily as her motions put her cleavage on display right before me. *So much for keeping it cool,* I thought, beads of sweat popping out across my forehead as I tried to hold her gaze. "Is it hot in here?" I queried, wiping the sweat off of my brow and removing my suit coat.

"Nope," she replied lightly, matching my gaze. "The temperature's just fine."

Looking for a distraction to keep me from simply grabbing and kissing her, I snatched a Fiji water bottle from my mini refrigerator, twisted off the cap and took a long swig.

The chilled liquid would hopefully cool me. As if on cue, I suddenly recalled London and our chance train encounter.

Though usually priding myself on my glibness, I'd found myself as tongue-tied with London as I suddenly felt with Pastor Patterson.

Maybe it had something to do with her killer curves; both women were stunningly attractive. With that thought, my mind trailed quickly into the gutter.

"Do I make you nervous?" she asked, jolting me back to the present.

"Of course not," I lied, wondering if my errant thoughts, probably spelled out across my face, had prompted her question. "I'm just hot."

"Has anyone ever told you that you have an amazing smile, Todd?"

"No," I responded cautiously, unsure where our conversation was leading.

"Well, let me be the first to tell you."

"Thank you," I conceded, still rather on edge.

"It makes you approachable," she continued. "That is a gift in many ways. It could be very helpful in the ministry." As she went on about the numerous ways to get involved in the church and 'use my gifts for God,' relaxation finally seeped into me.

Lulled by the smooth lilt of her voice, my focus was drifting.

Then, it happened.

Rising from my chair, I strode purposefully across the room to lock the door, feeling her gaze burning into me; now, it was time to make my move.

Walking up behind the chair, I placed my hands on her shoulders and gently massaged them.

"That feels great," she moaned, closing her eyes.

"Shh. Relax."

"Stop," she said as she rose and turned toward me, a smile curving her lips. She stepped closer, closed her eyes and leaned in.

I pulled her close and kissed her deep and hard.

She matched my kisses with passionate synchronicity. With one hand resting on the back of her neck, I reached up with the other, grabbed her ponytail and tugged.

"I like that, Todd," she moaned, breaking the kiss and staring deep into my eyes. Taking me by the hand, she led me to my executive chair and pushed me down. With a gleam in her eye, she raised her skirt and straddled me, sending waves of ecstasy surging through me.

Her unexpected actions were beyond hot, and I was ready.

"Todd, Todd."

I blinked a few times. I was alone in my chair, staring at Pastor Patterson across the desk. "Yes, Pastor?"

"Are you okay? You zoned out there for a few minutes. You don't have epilepsy, do you?"

"Oh! Oh God, no, I don't!" Now, I'd just used the Lord's name in vain. "I'm so sorry, excuse what I said. I didn't mean…"

"It's just a phrase, Todd. Even some people at church use it by accident. Anyway, you're fine. Really. But you're really all right? Not dizzy or something?"

"Yeah." I smiled, remembering the details of my daydream. "I mean no. I'm fine."

"It must have been quite a daydream," she laughed. "Now, as I was just asking, what kind of ministry work do you think would interest you most?"

Chapter 14

"T.B., YOU DIRTY DOG."

Blake and I were knocking back Hennessy shots inside the Violet Lounge, celebrating my recent victory over Amanda Pizzo for my client, William Gammon. I was too busy checking out all the fine ladies in the joint for his comment to register. "I thought we were boys," he added, putting me in a headlock and squeezed. "What's up with keeping secrets from your boy?"

"Listen, Blake," I choked out, disentangling myself from his kung fu grip. "I don't know what the hell you're talking about."

"Oh, so it's like that, huh?"

"Like what?"

"Rumor has it you are smashing both Pastor Patterson and that white girl with the blue eyes. You know, the one who looks like that actress, Megan Fox." He shot me a look that clearly conveyed his irritation at hearing this news secondhand.

"Even if these rumors were true," I countered, knocking back another shot. "Why would I tell you? Why tell anyone? It's not that big a deal, is it?"

"Bartender!" Blake called, slamming his fist down. "Because we're boys, that's why! You're my boy, I'm your boy. We don't keep secrets from each other, never have."

I'd always figured Blake for a wild card and normally, I wouldn't have thought twice about his accusations. But I couldn't understand why he, of all people, would be upset if I did happen to be sleeping with either of them. He was the one who'd encouraged me to find a woman in the church to sleep with in the first place, wasn't he?

While the rumors weren't true, the thought alone seemed to be pushing Blake over the edge.

Trying to diffuse what seemed to be a ticking time bomb, I turned to face him. "Look man, I'm not sleeping with either of them, but I may join the church."

"So it isn't true," he said, his voice ringing with relief. "I knew that no-good punk was lying."

"But what if it'd been true?" I joked. "What if I had been smashing the two of them?"

"Well, you're not," he stated with finality, signaling for yet another round of drinks. We each picked up a shot as Blake handed the bartender a one-hundred-dollar tip. "That's like asking me what if slavery never happened. It did!" He laughed, knocked back his shot and headed for the dance floor, picking up a brown-skinned cutie on the way.

As I watched him make a move on his latest conquest, my cell phone began vibrating in my pants pocket. Slipping the phone out and glancing at the screen, I quickly tossed a few bills on the bar and headed for the exit.

"Hey Mom," I answered, surprised to hear from her at such a late hour. "Is everything okay?"

"No, everything is not okay," she choked out. It sounded as though she had been crying.

"What's going on? What's wrong?"

"Your father just passed away."

Chapter 15

I STAGGERED INSIDE the crowded church, looking for familiar faces. It had been six days since I'd gotten the call. My sisters, Tena and Sade, were seated in the first pew. I made my way toward them, wondering if either of my brothers had shown up today.

"Hey," I greeted quietly. Neither responded, so without further exchange, I reluctantly took a seat directly in front of the golden casket housing my father's lifeless body.

"Where is Derek?" I whispered to Tena.

She just stared at me through dulled eyes and shrugged.

As I sat facing my father's casket, I tried to muster up a few emotions to add to the melancholy filling the small Baptist church around which I'd grown up. But all I could think was that there was a dead man in front of me who I barely knew, though his blood ran in my veins.

He wasn't exactly the kind of man people looked up to, not even his own children. Before my thoughts could spiral downward too dramatically, the pastor approached and grabbed me by the shoulder. "Are you ready, son?" he asked gently. I was glad I'd at least been given a heads up that I'd be called on to start the funeral service by sharing a few words about my father.

I took the three steps up to the pulpit and stepped behind the microphone.

As I tried to gather my thoughts, I scanned the crowd.

Droves of attendees were present, including a number of my father's ex-running mates.

Many of the old heads from his former crew were killers and ex-pimps and though my father hadn't been either, he'd hung with the likes of them. Wall-to-wall people were whispering, no doubt asking each other which of my father's sons I was.

From the pulpit, I turned toward a large wooden easel showcasing a life-sized portrait of my father at about thirty years old; the image was standing behind the casket.

Nice picture, I thought, trying to force a few tears from my eyes for show.

As I gave my speech, I caught myself wondering if anyone present actually believed the lies I was telling about the man who'd physically and mentally abused the woman who birthed me.

Chances were slim—I knew plenty about my father despite not actually having a relationship with him—but maybe someone in the audience had known a different side of him, beyond the sordid one that my own dark memories depicted. It was a hope to which my mind clung.

Despite my disdain for my father's abusive behavior toward my mother, as I spoke, I found my eyes repeatedly drawn to my father's widow. Seated in the front pew on the opposite side of the room from where I'd been seated, she was crying hysterically into a crumpled tissue.

A new sob echoed through the church with every false story tumbling from my lips.

Why had this woman chosen to be with a hard man like my father? But whatever her reasons, it was clear that her pain was real, her cries visceral and deeply upsetting.

She was obviously distraught over losing him. Playing the role of a good stepson, I concluded my accolades by rushing down from the pulpit to her side, seeking to comfort her with a hug.

Embracing me as if I were her own son, she sank her small face into my chest. Pulling back slightly, she looked up at me, but searching my face seemed to double her pain.

"Like your father," she whispered once, barely audible but filled with pain. "Your face shape." She traced my jawline with an index finger, and I closed my eyes as I felt it, her pain taking over my mind. He must have been a good man at least in some small way to have a woman feel so much for him. But as the therapist had told me too often, love was perplexing, complicated, a riddle, a constant puzzle without a solution, and a maze of sorry contradictions.

Some women just selected hard men to love, but it did not mean they would love the man any less for that. As the woman beside her pulled her away into another embrace, I lightly ran my fingers over the small wet spot her tears had left on the right lapel of my tan, pinstripe suit.

Then I traced the outline of my own jaw. *This is all I have in common with my father?*

It didn't come as any surprise. Perhaps it was more enlightening to hear there was any similarity at all, any tiny thing that connected us identifiably in the eyes of others. They saw more of a connection than I had ever done, even in that small likeness between us both.

Suddenly, it hit me that my father was really gone. While he hadn't been much of a father to me, no longer would I hear the three simple words he loved to preach. "Live your life," he told me whenever we talked. We hadn't spoken often, but standing there next to his weeping widow, his echoing words cut straight through my heart. *Live your life. Live your life.*

"My father loved you," I heard myself say to the woman when next she broke away from the hug of the woman seated on her other side. "He thought the world of you. And he was lucky to have you." I leaned toward her, bringing her frail body in toward mine, hugging her close.

Against all my usual inclinations, I planted a small kiss atop her head. Public affection to a stranger never came easy to me, but on this occasion, it seemed the right thing to do, and I was sure she would remember it and think back on it as some small measure of comfort.

What else was there? The man I'd known had been a snake, one of the meanest men I'd ever encountered, but there'd never been any doubt my stepmother loved him, and he her in his way.

Now, she was without the man with whom she had spent the past twenty-five years.

Having known a very different side of him, I couldn't relate to her pain, but she deserved her time to grieve. It came back to me that my stint at the pulpit was over; I'd had enough of the lies. But it had been good to comfort my dad's widow, a nice woman as far as I could tell.

However, I was free now, free to carry on my day however I wished.

As I made my way back toward my sisters, I looked toward the rear of the room, finally spotting my mother, also crying. Did her tears have anything to do with the blatant lies I'd just spread from the pulpit about the kind of man my father was? Or was it possible she really missed him? It didn't matter either way. As her gaze caught mine, I offered her a supportive smile.

Taking my seat, my glance dropped again to my sisters, wondering what they thought of my speech. Their faces were impassive. Tena had hidden her eyes behind a large pair of dark sunglasses and Sade was sitting stock-still, staring forward blankly.

As the service continued, Tena also stepped to the podium to share a few words. Listening to her go on about our father's accomplishments and legacy, her lies seemed even more blatant than my own. Any stranger in the room would have thought this deceased man was about to receive a father-of-the-year award. Though Tena had worked tremendously hard to overcome the same tough childhood I'd endured, she credited our father for much of her success, including the master's degree she'd recently earned in journalism. It was all nonsense.

Deciding I'd heard enough, I stopped listening and turned toward Henry, my oldest brother, who had arrived at some point during my speech. He was seated a little way down the pew from me. Dressed in dark slacks and a wool blazer, he had aged a bit since the last time I'd seen him.

Beside him was his longtime girlfriend, Janet. There was no doubt Henry was madly in love with Janet, but I'd always thought she was bipolar for the hell she put him through.

Seeing her left a sour taste in my mouth, but I wanted my brother to be happy, surely?

And as far as I could tell, Janet seemed to be the source of his happiness.

It seemed Henry didn't care for the lies spewing from the pulpit either. As I studied him down the row, the scathing look on his face mirrored my own.

Why do people always have nice things to say about the dead?

I wondered. *They never manage a decent word about them when they're still breathing, do they?*

Hardly anyone had ever possessed a single nice word to say about my father while he was alive, but now that he was gone, he might as well have been Gandhi.

As Tena finally finished glorifying our father and returned to her seat, the minister, an older, light-skinned man, stepped up to preach a heartfelt sermon on love and forgiveness.

His power and conviction were beyond impressive, but my mind was reeling with too many conflicting thoughts and feelings to really appreciate his message.

As the service finally concluded, my father's siblings, Clarence and Joann, were standing in the aisle, Joann bawling into Clarence's shoulder. It hurt me to see her crying the way she did, but instead of rushing forward to console her as I had with my stepmother, I stayed back.

Clarence awkwardly moved himself to escort her down the aisle toward the casket and portrait to say goodbye. My father's closed casket request… What was it all about?

But as usual during his lifetime, he'd gotten what he asked for. In life, no one would ever go against him, and it seemed to have played out just the same in death.

My father had made it clear—and had made my sisters promise to see it through—that he wanted a closed casket funeral so no one would see him in his final state.

They had pushed him on it, arguing that we'd all want one last look at him, but he'd remained insistent. It was his death, and he'd die it his own way.

Now, in his absence, his wishes stood. The casket would remain closed.

With the heavy swirl of emotions filling the church, was I supposed to quietly mourn in remembrance like most of the attendees were doing? Or should I weep alongside my family?

Neither seemed right, so I simply sat there, motionless in my seat, until the funeral crowd slowly trickled out the back of the sanctuary. Only as the very last person exited the double doors did I finally rise to follow the procession to the grave site.

Chapter 16

AS THE PASTOR shared a graveside message on repentance, I wiped away Mom's tears with the hanky from my coat pocket. "He's in a much better place now, Mom," I murmured, surprising myself with a few tears of my own.

"Oh, believe me, he is not in a better place," she replied, more firmly than I expected. "He is exactly where his slimy ass deserves to be, in the ground with all the other maggots and worms."

Her eyes were hard and unforgiving despite her tears.

"Shh, Mom," I whispered as I patted her arm gently, trying to avoid drawing attention to us as the pastor continued.

Inside, I smiled slightly at her words and the courage it took to say them.

"No more lies," she proclaimed loudly and tossed her white rose on top of my father's casket. "Good riddance, you asshole," she added for good measure. Her unexpected comment echoed clearly through the crowd, bringing more than a few heads whipping around toward us.

Even the pastor's eyes widened in surprise, though he managed not to stumble over his words.

Henry, who had been crying on Janet's shoulder, heard the commotion and hurried toward us, panic all over his face. "What's wrong with Mom?" He stared me down.

"I don't know." I shrugged. Noticing the scene, Tena and Sade approached us as well, wrapping their arms around Mom and guiding her away from Henry and me, encouraging her to stand with them for support. As they stepped away, Henry made his way back to Janet.

I remained where I was, glad to be left alone for the moment. Deep down, my siblings and I all knew why Mom had vilified our father as we'd lain his body to rest.

He hadn't been any kind of stand-up man, especially to Mom, but we were grown now, having moved on from our painful past. It must have been more difficult for Mom to do the same with all the pain he'd inflicted on her verbally and physically over the years. From where I stood, it was still sharp and deep enough to incite a graveside scene, even all these years later.

Finally, the pastor concluded his message and invited everyone present to close the service by joining together in the hymn 'Amazing Grace.'

After the service, I dutifully stood alongside Mom and my siblings, shaking hands and accepting condolences. As I thanked several people who said they would pray for me and my family, Mom's eyes were still following me.

"Your mother has every right to be upset with your father," his widow pronounced, appearing suddenly at my side. "What he made her do is unforgivable. It changed your family forever."

"Yeah, I know," I said. "It wasn't right." His abusiveness had been no secret.

"I know it hardly helps now, but I want you to know I'm so sorry he made your mother give up your twin brother at birth. I'm sorry for you, and sorry for your poor mother."

I stared at her in disbelief for a moment.

"He did what?" I asked dumbly, waiting for her words to sink in. As they did, each one struck into me as if a physical blow, knocking me backwards.

I spun toward my mother, shock and horror rippling through my body.

My father's widow quickly realized she'd spoken out of turn; her eyes widened, and her jaw dropped as she raised her fingers to her lips. "I'm so sorry," she repeated. "You didn't know?"

Her comments didn't even register.

"I have a twin brother?" I shouted toward my siblings in anger.

I looked at my mother with tears in my eyes. "Mom." I grabbed her hand, searching her face for the truth. "Tell me it isn't true. Do I have a twin brother?"

"Yes," she cried, clutching my hand as tears poured down her cheeks.

I nearly crumbled, overwhelmed by this unforgivable revelation, but Mom held me firmly.

Tears fell readily as I mourned the terrible loss of an entire relationship, a completely different life, one I'd never had a chance to know.

"We couldn't afford to take care of the two of you." She tried to comfort me. "I had no choice. Your father made me give him up for adoption. I'm so sorry, Todd."

Grief and guilt bit at my psyche. *They gave him away. They kept me. It could have been me though. What kind of a life might I have had? Would I have been in and out of group homes or would a loving couple have taken me? What has my brother endured while I've been held safe?*

Unable to face my family while processing it all, I stood, robotically wiped my face, and walked to my car without looking back, though they called out to me.

As I reached over to open the car door, a familiar voice reached my ears.

"Todd! Wait a moment!" Pastor Patterson was waving frantically in my direction.

"What are you doing here?" My voice was flat, numb. She rushed toward me.

"I called your office last week." She wrapped her arms around my waist and stared deep into my eyes. "Judy said your father passed away. I felt I needed to be here."

Accepting her support, my tears fell on her shoulder.

"I'm here for you, Todd," she said solemnly, then kissed me on the cheek. "I will *always* be here for you."

Chapter 17

"I CAN'T BELIEVE this. Why do they keep doing this to me?" I cried out to no one in particular.

"Who, Todd?" asked Dr. Perry from her usual chair across from me.

"All of them." The tears were welling. "I don't understand why they can't see me, doc. I might as well be invisible for all they care."

"Try taking a deep breath, Todd," she suggested. "Tell me. Who do you feel can't see you?"

"My family, that's who!" I set off sniffing loudly, my nose

running. "I'm invisible to every one of them. The whole lot; I've never counted."

She grabbed a box of Kleenex from the nearby bookshelf and offered it my way. Grabbing a single tissue, I blew my nose and immediately reached for another to wipe my eyes.

The relentless crying carried on until she handed me the box. "Just hang onto the box."

"I'm sorry, doc," I apologized.

"Sorry for what?"

I lifted the tear-filled tissue in response. "Going through all your supplies!"

It was a brief interlude of humor in the moment.

"Your emotions are real," she assured me. "There's no need to apologize for that. And for the record, you are capable of being loved."

Her words touched me, and I felt something small and tight unravel just a bit inside my chest. Hearing it aloud, it was clear she was right, that nothing stopped me being loved.

So why the hell doesn't my family see that? I wondered. *And why do I still feel as though I don't really deserve it?*

There was so much baggage to unpack, but that was why I was here.

Looking up, I met Dr. Perry's steady gaze. Now or never, I told myself. I took a deep breath, then let it out slowly. "You're right," I said finally. "I think I'm ready."

"Ready for what?"

"You know, to lay it all on the table, to bare my soul to you. For you to help me figure it all out. That's what therapists do, right? It's what you offered me some time back."

"Okay, I'm listening."

"All right, here it goes. Since the last time I was here, my father died. His funeral was earlier this week."

"I'm so sorry to hear about the passing of your father," she said, emotion flitting across her usually impassive face. "Were you close to your father?"

"No. I didn't really know him."

"When did you last see him? What is your last memory of him?" She opened her padfolio and prepared to take notes.

"It's a long story," I said, hedging. "Are you sure you have time?"

"You are my last appointment today. I'm all ears."

"Well, we talked a few times on the phone after he and Mom divorced and he remarried, but my last in-person memory of him is from a lot farther back. The last time I actually saw my father, I was six years old." I glanced at her, trying to gauge her reaction.

"Please continue."

I lay back on the couch and thought back to that fateful night that changed me forever.

*****

I'd woken in the middle of the night, maybe around one o'clock, something like that. Falling back to sleep was impossible, so instead of lying there staring at nothing, I crept down from the top bunk and tiptoed past my older brothers, Henry and Derek, both asleep in their beds.

I wanted to sneak a snack from the kitchen, maybe some milk and cookies, even though we were never allowed to do that.

As I made my way past my two brothers, my stomach let out an enormous roar! Well, I was sure it would wake one or both of them. I stood there frozen, hoping and praying that Henry, the family dictator, hadn't heard the grumbling. He didn't move, but Derek rolled over.

He cracked open one of his eyes and stared directly at me. I was in for it now; Derek was only slightly less terrifying than Henry. I opened my mouth to explain to him what I was doing up so late, but before I said anything, he rolled back over and started snoring.

I was safe for the moment, but instead of satisfying my cookies and milk craving, I hustled back to the top of the bunk and pretended to sleep, just in case. I lay there quietly, but there was such a deep rage at my brothers. Here I was, barely six years old and already completely terrorized by them. Instead of protecting me, they bullied me every chance they got.

Still awake and starving at 4:15 a.m., I climbed back down from my bed a second time and quietly made my way toward the kitchen for my snack.

This time, I didn't care who I woke up.

Before I could make it to the kitchen, a key rattled in the front door of our apartment, so I hid around the corner in the hall-way. The door opened, and it was my father standing there in the doorway—or swaying there, I should say—but he didn't see me, being way too engrossed, stumbling and knocking things over, drunk and high out of his mind.

A twisted, sick feeling was starting in my stomach as I watched him. Even at six, it was so clear what it meant when he got drunk. Every time he did, he would beat Mom. We didn't witness it but we heard it, and the next day, she'd be bruised all over and hurting, and weeping.

And every time, it seemed as if it got worse. It wasn't even as if there was anyone for me to talk to about it. Anyway, this time, I had to act quickly, so ran back to my room.

I shook Derek and Henry, willing them to get up. Derek responded first, rubbing the sleep out of his eyes, and rising to his feet, towering above me.

He stared down at me, anger rolling off him. Grabbing me by my shirt collar, he pulled me toward him, nearly lifting me off my feet. "Do you know what time it is?" he demanded.

"Otis is home. And he's drunk!" I cried out. He let go of my shirt and began pacing around the bedroom, naked from his waist up and just wearing a pair of baggy long sleep pants tied at the waist. He was punching at the wall with bare knuckles, cursing.

With this fracas, Henry was soon awake too.

"Not again," Henry moaned as he sat on the edge of his bed and rested his face in his hands for a moment before meeting Derek's eyes. The foreboding look they shared reinforced what I already knew: that poor Mom was about to take another beating.

It was the second time in as many nights that our father had stumbled home drunk and high. "What the hell's he doing here?" Derek blurted.

"I don't know, man," Henry answered nervously. He cracked open the bedroom door to see what was going on, tiptoeing to place his eye against the gap.

"He's on the floor," he reported soon. "He's got a lit cigarette dangling from his mouth so if he doesn't kill Mom, he'll probably burn us all to death."

It should have sounded funny, should have raised a laugh among the three of us but it did not. We were all scared of our father, and I was terrified of my two bullying brothers almost as much.

*****

"It's not even part of the story," I said, glancing at Dr. Perry, breaking the flow of my tale, "but you have to understand our father was a smooth country boy from the south. He was tall, handsome and we all knew he repeatedly cheated on Mom with white women. We didn't have much at home, but he always managed to wear the finest clothes money could buy and cruise around town in a two-door forest green Lincoln Continental.

"To any stranger, it would've looked like our father had it going on."

"I think I know the type," she replied supportively. "Please, go on with your story."

I closed my eyes again, picking up where I left off.

"It's probably where I get my love of good clothing brands.

Like, I always notice the brands people wear. Stupid really, I know it is."

The fact was incidental, but in the moment, felt like something I ought to say.

"I noticed that," Madison said. "That you always talk about the brands. It's all right."

*****

As Henry, Derek and I peered out of our bedroom door, Dad lay paralyzed on the floor for a few minutes. Then, he yelled toward Mom's bedroom.

"Woman, get your lazy ass out here now!"

We all watched as Mom's bedroom door slowly opened. She glanced our way and saw the three of us staring at her with tears in our eyes. She was tearful too, probably more so because she knew her kids were seeing all of this and knew exactly what was going on.

I remember she motioned for us to go back to bed, but how could we? We knew the man who'd fathered her five children was now about to beat her in front of us.

Without hesitation, she approached our father and even in that moment, refused to show fear.

"What took you so long to get here?" he shouted at her, reaching up and punching her in the mouth. We watched her use the back of her hand to wipe the trickle of blood away from the corner of her lips and when she brought her hand away, it was all red and more blood just came out afterward, so it'd been pointless anyway. She needed to spit it out but wouldn't.

"I didn't hear you come in," she told him calmly. And the more she talked, the more the blood ran down her bottom lip and off the tip of her chin. It was horrible and I felt sick just seeing it.

Ignoring her answer, he asked, "What the hell are you wearing?" Mom had on a long white cotton nightgown and brown slippers. Her hair was pinned up neatly in a bun.

I just thought she looked like an angel who had come down from heaven.

*****

"She didn't deserve his anger," I asserted, feeling the memory poignantly.

"Of course not. No person ever deserves this cruelty. Go on," encouraged Dr. Perry.

*****

"Baby, you need to go to bed," she encouraged him. He rose to his feet, swaying back and forth. She looked over at the three of us. Her lip was swelling and her eyes flooding with tears. I was so angry to see Mom defenseless. I wanted my father dead so he could never hurt her again.

As she turned back to face him, he exploded. "You don't tell me what to do or where to go, woman!" he yelled, shoving her so violently that she fell to the living room floor.

I guess that's when she started to fear for her life because Mom got up from the floor and began frantically running through our small apartment, screaming for help.

Terrified, we closed and locked our bedroom door, but could still hear everything. Henry, just about thirteen at the time, slowly cracked the door back open and we all saw our father's dark eyes shift toward us. He knew we were all awake, but it didn't stop him from slapping Mom around. It seemed to make it worse, as if he liked having an audience.

I felt helpless being so small. Derek tried to push his way through the door to help Mom, but Henry held him back by the collar of his shirt, telling both of us to 'be quiet and keep still.'

The three of us watched as Mom took every punch and slap our father threw until her beautiful and angelic face was covered in blood. She still wouldn't cry or beg.

By this time, our father had his knee pressed against Mom's neck. He reached inside his brown leather jacket and removed a chrome .38-caliber pistol. We recognized it as the same one he usually kept stored away in the living room closet inside a rugged old safety box.

I don't know why he had it in his pocket that night, but he was threatening to kill Mom if she didn't stop screaming. Eventually, Mom stopped fighting and she seemed to be giving up which scared me even more, but then her lips were moving, and she set off praying, 'Jesus help me'.

Of course, I'd heard about this guy Jesus at church and Mom called out to him often, but every time, Jesus never showed up for her, did he? He left her fending for herself, suffering.

I remember wondering who this guy was and why he never bothered helping when she asked.

As we watched our father continue to yell at her, throwing punches every few moments, the door across the hallway to our sisters' room cracking open as well.

My oldest sister, Sade, and my other sister, Tena, were holding one another and crying. Sade whispered toward the three of us, something I'll never forget.

"Do something before he kills her!" she demanded.

But what could we do? We were only kids.

How could we stop a man over six feet tall, drunk and violent?

I remember looking toward my older brothers for help, hoping they'd do something in response to my sister's plea. Derek cracked his knuckles and slammed his fist down on the bed; I could tell he was ready to make a move.

"We'll have to do something," he said to Henry.

"Like what?" Henry whispered.

"I don't know, but we have to stop him before he kills Mom!" he shouted. Then, he grabbed his aluminum baseball bat and stormed out of the room. When he reached the living room, he swung it at our father's head. "Get off my mother!" he yelled. "Right now!"

"Are we going to help him?" I asked Henry since he was the oldest.

In response, he pushed me down to the floor. I stared up and told him, "Instead of beating on me, you need to help Derek."

Out in the living room, Derek gripped the handle of the baseball bat tighter and looked our father straight in the eye. "You ever put your hands on my mother again," he said, "And I'm going to kill you, you no-good coward!"

"Little niggah got heart, huh?" He laughed and then in the meanest tone he could find, he said, "Boy, if you don't get your little ass back in that room, I'm going to whip you like you stole something."

Derek didn't budge and I found a whole new level of respect for him at that moment. I don't know how, but he wasn't shaken by our father's menacing threat. In fact, he challenged him again.

"Do it, then!" Derek shouted with tears in his eyes. "I'm not afraid of you—not anymore!"

Out of nowhere, our father began to laugh.

He knew as well as we did that Derek didn't stand a chance against him, but Derek's bravery encouraged the rest of us to stand up to him too. We all rushed out of our bedrooms with any weapon we could find, forming a protective circle around Mom.

Seeing all of us there, willing to fight... I don't know, maybe it was too much for him. Or maybe it was a reality check or something. Either way, he leaned back to eye each of us for a long moment before slipping his gun back into his pocket.

Looking over our heads, he smiled devilishly at Mom.

"I'll be back," he threatened, grabbing his keys. Then, without another word, he walked out of the front door. I remember wanting him to die, maybe for a car to hit him, so he could never come back. We all helped Mom up from the floor and she held onto Derek tightly as she cried like we'd never seen her cry before. Seeing the blood and bruises all over Mom's face and body made me cry too. All I wanted to know was why. Why

did the man who was my father beat the only woman I'd ever loved? What was her crime?

"Don't worry, Mom. I'm going to kill him," Derek promised. "One day, I promise. I'm going to kill him. I'll bash his head in. Then, he can never hurt you again."

"Stop talking foolish, boy," Mom told him. "That's your father you're talking about."

She wiped the tears from Derek's eyes with a corner of her nightgown as she cupped his face with her other hand. "No matter what your father does to me or anyone else, he is still your father and you all should honor him. It's what Jesus asks us to do."

It was a line we'd heard before, but after such a severe beating, Mom had to be crazy to think any one of us would honor that man, no matter who was requesting it. I'd never heard such a stupid thing in my whole life! Not from anyone.

Besides, I'd seen her pray to this Jesus so many times and she'd gotten nothing in return.

I figured if what we'd just witnessed was what we could expect from this Jesus by following in Mom's footsteps, I wanted no part of it.

He hadn't helped the most beautiful person in my life, so why would he possibly help me?

The rest of that night, the five of us stayed up and cared for Mom. Derek slept in front of the front door with his aluminum bat by his side. Henry was swinging a pair of nunchucks over his shoulder as if he thought he must be Bruce Lee.

Sade and Tena were lying in Mom's arms, crying as if they'd never stop.

I didn't know what to do or who to console, so I leaned against the living room wall, trying to look tough as I watched everyone from a distance.

The next day, Mom packed all of our things and we moved.

*****

"We never saw our father again, not even at his funeral," I told Dr. Perry. "The casket was closed."

Drained and depleted, it dawned on me that my story might have been different if my twin brother had been there, and a painful wave of emotions rose within me again.

"I should also tell you about my twin brother…"

I began to speak again, but Madison held up a hand, stopping me.

She placed her padfolio on the small table next to her chair, folded her arms across her chest and stared at me.

"First, Todd, tell me, how many sessions have you and I had together?"

"Huh?" Her question caught me off guard. After spilling my guts, I couldn't see how this was remotely relevant, but played along with it. "You asked me to come every week, but I know I haven't been consistent. I believe this is our sixth or seventh session. Why?"

She rose from her seat and came to perch near me on the couch. "You are an incredible man, Todd. You are a lot stronger than you think."

"Thanks, but what are you getting at, doc?"

"You are definitely capable of being loved, Todd," she said, repeating her earlier comment. "Your family doesn't see you because they cannot see themselves."

I paused, trying to follow. "Okay… I'm confused."

"To a degree, we are all products of our environment. You are no different than the rest of us, only that your environment was a tough one. But here is where you get to make a choice. Will you remain in the past and become a casualty of it? Or will you leave the past behind and move forward? It's time to see yourself through your eyes, not your family's. Don't you think?

"For you to move on, you must begin the forgiveness process, to forgive not just those who have let you down, but yourself too, Todd. Until you're able to release the pain and anger you've been carrying for so long, you will never be free. You are holding yourself captive to the past."

"Of course I want to escape my past. That's why I'm here, doc," I replied, feeling as though that part was obvious. "But what's all this about forgiveness?" I asked in a frustrated tone. "I wouldn't be here if they hadn't done what they did. I blame every one of them."

"What are you blaming them for?"

"For not being there for me."

"Maybe they weren't, but have you been there for them?"

Damn, I thought as I processed her question. *I guess I haven't really shown up for them either, but still...* That old familiar feeling of blame was back again. I wasn't good enough.

Now, even my therapist was inadvertently telling me she was tired of hearing me whining on. But this was the story of my life; I was always the one in the wrong, no matter how hard I tried.

"Why does it feel as if you are blaming me?" I asked. "What did I do wrong?"

I slumped against the couch, feeling the weight of it all. "I give up."

"No, Todd." She rose to her feet. "I am not blaming you. And a tough question being posed does not entitle you to say you give up. But what I am asking you to do is look closely at your life, to take stock of all that you already have and to determine what role you want the past to play in your present. As you've told me, you are a successful attorney.

"You have great friends too, Todd. In our last session, you said you'd even met the *one*, the perfect woman for you—even though you allowed her to escape your grasp."

"No! She got away. She wouldn't even give me her last name," I protested.

"So that's it? You're willing to let her go, just like that? Why didn't you stay on the train? Why didn't you try harder, go after what you wanted?"

"Not making this easy, are you?" I shot her a half-smile, figuring I probably needed whatever it was she'd decided to dish out.

"Prior to today, I only knew about your life as it is currently. Now I know something about your past too. With this fuller story, I understand you better, Todd. And I need you to know that if you are going to move forward, it is essential for you to remain true to yourself.

"If you forgive and let go of the heaviness you've carried for so long, you'll find it's okay to accept all the goodness in your life. Or you can stay where you are, resenting life and feeling like a perpetual victim. It's time to look in the mirror and decide whether you see yourself…

"Or your father."

She made me recoil with those words. They disgusted me.

"Never!" I snapped back. "I will never be like him."

"Then stop making excuses and start living your life. You have so much already; what else do you want? If you haven't found happiness on your own, perhaps it's time to get some new support. You mentioned you'd been visiting a church; maybe it's time to try again."

"Church," I laughed. "Like that will help. If God didn't protect my mother, why would He care about me? I gave up on God a long time ago, doc."

"All right, then I have just one more question for you: What do you want from me? What are you hoping I will give you that you don't already have? If you've already decided not even God can fix your problems, then what is the point in listening to me?"

She pinned me with a pointed stare before standing and walking over to open her office door.

For a moment longer, I sat frozen on the couch; I had no answer for her, and she knew it.

Frustrated, I grabbed my car keys from the side table and headed toward the exit, still trying to piece together everything she'd said.

Chapter 18

I DIDN'T LEAVE MY apartment for the next few weeks; the phone had been switched to silent shortly after leaving my father's gravesite, but the scene I'd made just beforehand had sent a pretty clear message to family and friends that I wanted to be left alone. Even now, weeks later, just thinking about the fact that I'd been separated from my twin brother at birth twisted my gut.

Anger was on the rise in me yet again, a deep burning and gnawing in my gut. Why didn't anyone tell me I had a twin brother? Where could he be? Was he looking for me? Was he even alive? I had no answers, no leads and nowhere to go... just an agonizing need to find out.

Finding solace the only way I knew how, I was out on the balcony sipping on a Corona and smoking a Black & Mild when a black Audi A5 convertible pulled into the parking lot below.

Nice car, I thought as I chugged down the rest of the beer. An attractive woman wearing workout clothes and a baseball cap climbed out. She seemed lost.

One of my neighbors was dumping his trash when she approached him. "Could you tell me where Todd Banks lives?" Her voice floated up to my balcony.

He turned and pointed up at me. "Right there, ma'am."

"Oh! Thank you." She headed my way, removing her baseball cap and smiling up at me, squinting as she looked toward the bright sky.

It was Pastor Patterson.

"Hi, Todd." She waved. "Where have you been?"

I quickly tucked my beer bottle behind the support post of the balcony and put out the Black & Mild. "Hey, Pastor." I waved back. "I'll be down in a minute."

I was in no way ready for company, but dashed to the bathroom to brush my teeth and wash my face. After applying deodorant and swapping out my dirty loungewear for clean clothes, I headed out to meet my stalker. *How does she keep finding me?*

I was both irritated and impressed at her determination and skills.

"Where have you been?" she demanded again, hugging me tightly. "Everyone's worried about you."

"There's no need to be. I'm good." I shot her a half smile.

"What are you doing today?" she asked excitedly.

"I don't have any plans," I replied, trying to keep my voice light. I glanced toward my balcony and spotted my Corona bottle hanging off the edge. I quickly shifted my eyes back to hers, hoping her gaze hadn't followed mine.

"Good." She grabbed my hand and led me to her car. "We're going for a ride."

After three weeks of nothing but my own swirling thoughts about my lost brother, I had to admit I was happy to see Pastor Patterson. I had no idea what she had up her sleeve, but I was already buoyed by her enthusiasm and decisiveness.

I figured she was exactly what I needed.

"Where are you taking me?" I asked, fastening my seatbelt.

She flashed a brilliant smile. "You'll see when we get there."

Just under an hour later, we pulled into a shopping center and parked in front of a sign reading 'Porsche's Salon.' "We're here," she said. I raised my eyebrow in return.

The door chimed as we walked in. "Hey, ladies," she greeted.

"Hey, Pastor!" Everyone rang out in unison.

"Everyone, this is my friend Todd." She slipped her fingers into mine and squeezed as she began making introductions. "Todd, this is my girl, Riley." Riley looked like an Egyptian princess, brown-skinned with long curly black hair and a body to die for.

She greeted me with a perfect smile. "Nice to meet you, Todd."

"You too," I said, returning her smile.

Next, was Sydney, the owner of Porsche's Salon and a Ciara look-alike with stunning brown eyes. "What's up?" she intoned. I nodded but didn't speak; she seemed to look through me.

Was I invisible?

"And this is Angie, also known as G."

Oozing confidence, Angie was clearly the outspoken one of the group. Tall, dark-skinned and sexy as hell, she greeted me with a raised fist reminiscent of the Black Panther Party. "Looking good, Todd." She winked at me. I smiled back.

"These are my girls," Pastor Patterson concluded as she took a seat in Sydney's chair.

"So, Todd." Angie approached me. "How do you know the pastor?"

"Don't mind her, Todd," Pastor Patterson laughed. "Leave my friend alone, G."

"We're not in church, Pastor," she scolded back. "This is my domain. I just want to get to know the brother."

"We met at church," I said.

Across from where Pastor Patterson sat, Riley was braiding the hair of a young girl sporting a private school uniform. "So, Todd," she asked casually. "What do you do for a living?"

"I work in Cambridge."

"Doing what?" Angie interrupted.

"He's an attorney," Pastor Patterson chimed in.

"What kind of attorney is he?"

All eyes pivoted toward me. "I'm a criminal attorney," I clarified.

As their barrage of questions began, not least that same old one about how I could possibly defend these heinous guilt-laden perpetrators, I settled into an empty chair. Over the next two hours, I filled them in on my history, grateful for the distraction from my more recent ordeals.

I didn't know why Pastor Patterson had thought a trip to a hair salon would be good for me, but as I got to know the women of Porsche's Salon, I discovered they were more than just beautiful and successful. They were women of character and integrity, and I appreciated their perspectives.

Chapter 19

I'D GIVEN UP on pestering my family for details about my brother. Whether they knew nothing or were simply refusing to speak up didn't matter; they'd let me down and betrayed me.

Instead, I sulked about it until Henry stopped by my apartment.

Then, I decided to let the cat out the bag.

"Listen, little bruh." He locked his bear claw around my wrist. "You've moped around long enough. I think it's time you knew the truth."

"I'm listening," I said, stone-faced.

"Your twin brother's name is Khalil Gilliam." He removed a wrinkled photograph from his wallet and handed it to me. "And he is no choir boy."

"Damn." I looked up. "He looks just like me!"

"Looks like," he emphasized, grabbing a beer from the refrigerator. "He's nothing like you."

"What do you mean?"

"Our brother Khalil is the devil," Henry stated before taking a long swig of his beer. He snatched the picture out of my hand. "I shouldn't even be telling you this; you're better off without him. We all are. He's as mean as they come."

"Yeah, whatever, man." I dismissed his theory. "Tell me about him. What does he do for a living? Where does he live? Does he have any children?"

"If you want to know so badly, why not just ask him yourself?" Henry replied. He slid the picture back inside his wallet. "You didn't hear it from me, but he'll be at Johnson Brothers' Warehouse in an hour. But before you go…" He paused to chug the rest of his beer and cocked his eyebrow. "Are you sure you want to go down this road?"

"I am," I responded resolutely. My eyes were wide, hardly able to take in that I'd get to see him so soon, having only just found out about his existence.

"Get dressed and I'll take you to meet our brother." He grabbed another Corona from the refrigerator. "Remember though," he called, popping the top as I headed down the hallway to my room. "You asked for this!"

*****

We rode in silence for about an hour before arriving at Johnson Brothers' Warehouse. As we pulled up and parked near an inconspicuous door, it seemed unbelievable that I was moments away from meeting my long-lost brother. This was something straight out of a movie.

"Take this." Henry pressed a small pistol into my hands.

"What for?" I asked.

"For protection," he said tersely, inserting a clip into his gun. "And please don't shoot yourself with it," he laughed.

"You know I don't like firearms, right?" I stated, shooting him a sideways glance.

"Yup, but you better get acquainted with that one, at least. Because like father, like son."

I knew what he meant, never forgetting the time Dad had brandished the shooter at us.

He stood and slipped his gun into his holster. Bracing his hands on the doorframe, he leaned back into the car. "Cain and Abel is a true story," he said, giving me a long look.

Henry's words and cryptic expression were foreboding enough to send chills up my spine. I wanted to know my brother, my twin, but definitely didn't feel good about bringing guns into the mix. Suddenly, meeting Khalil didn't seem like such a good idea after all.

"Todd!" Henry's bark brought my eyes back to his. "Last chance. Sure you want to do this?"

I took a deep breath. "Yeah," I said, trying to shove down my uncertainty. "I'm sure."

"All right. Let me go check it out. Then, I'll come back and get you."

I nodded my agreement, grateful for the few extra moments to collect myself. As Henry made his way toward the building, I glanced at the dash clock. 11:48 a.m.

By 12:15 p.m., I was too antsy to wait any longer, and would go find out what the holdup was. Gun in hand, locked and loaded, I cautiously approached the warehouse with every sense on high alert. Slowly, I crept through the doors, intent on entering with no mishaps.

Success. Yet I should not have been so cocky, so sure of myself, so blasé.

This was my worst nightmare.

The smell that hit me on entry was that of iron, a stench that was unmistakable. Even if you hadn't come across it before, there was only one thing it could be. Blood, human blood, and plenty of it. Sure enough, just a few feet away, hogtied and lying in the pool of semi-congealed ruby wetness was Henry, a deep gash over his eye, surely close to bleeding out.

There have to be more wounds than just that one. I was assessing all the blood he'd lost.

I ran to his side and shook him gently. "Henry, Henry," I whispered, afraid of the covert assailant, wherever the attacker may be now. He felt slightly warm, though his skin was pallid.

He groaned, the kind of low moan of a man who wanted to be left to himself.

My brother's eyes cracked open, and I let out a huge breath of relief. "What bastard did this to you?" I demanded, pulling out my pocketknife and quickly cutting through all his ties.

The feel of cold, hard metal on the back of my head froze me in my tracks.

"I did it," rang out the cold voice behind me. Dropping my pocketknife on the concrete, I raised my hands into the air as slow as I could. Panic and cold fear oozed from every pore. My hands trembled and my voice was unsteady, barely over a whisper too, just like Henry's.

"D-don't shoot," I pleaded.

"Turn around," he ordered. "Slowly."

Closing my eyes, I took a deep breath and pivoted to face my brother's attacker. Cautiously, I cracked open my eyes. My jaw dropped. For an instant, it was just like staring into a mirror.

"Who the hell are you?" he asked, incredulity all over his face. Our resemblance was far too obvious to miss. Perhaps, for the first time in my life, my genetics were working for me.

I took another deep breath, trying to slow my racing pulse.

"My name's Todd Banks." My eyes locked on his gun. "I believe I'm your twin brother."

Our likeness was incredible, but we were nothing alike. Khalil, I was very quickly learning, didn't seem to care for anything or anyone, except himself. I watched him closely as he paced back and forth, processing my announcement with his finger still on the trigger.

"Shit!" he yelled out, filled with vitriol at the world, kicking out at the floor, the walls. He cursed far worse words I would never dream of, let alone think to repeat.

"Listen," I said bluntly, wanting to cut to the chase and get out of there as quickly as possible. "Up until our father's funeral, I didn't even know you existed. The only reason I came here today was to see the truth for myself. I came to meet you, brother."

The word *brother* turned my guts inside out.

He stopped pacing and faced me but uttered not a word. His eyes were cold and hard as he stared. I forced my breathing to slow as best I could, having to get a grip on my nerves. *Insecure, insecure* rang out in my skull, Madison's words. I had to be in control now.

Have to be a man. Have to have courage and self-belief. I stared back.

"Well, you shouldn't be here," he finally replied, icy. "There are some things that should stay buried." His voice was sinister. "Even if we are brothers," he said and laughed grimly, "the world that I live in is far from the polarized life that you clearly live. Well, yours is a nice life, I'd say, looking at you. A pretty boy, aren't you? See, good haircut. Good clothes. *Money.*"

He eyed me up and down. "My advice to you, brother, is to stay the hell away from me… Otherwise, you may find yourself eulogized."

Before I could respond, Khalil turned on his heel, crossed the room in three steps and was gone.

Chapter 20

"PRAISE THE LORD, CHURCH."

"Hallelujah."

"I said, praise the Lord, church!" she shouted louder.

"Hallelujah!" bellowed the church in unison.

Despite having told myself I wanted nothing to do with the church, for the second week in a row, Pastor Patterson's mastery of stage and performance had somehow captivated me.

She was the Pied Piper, and the congregants were her entranced followers.

The way she commanded the room was a sight to behold.

As I sat in the front pew admiring her prowess, she locked eyes with me and winked, reminding me so much of the look London had given me on the train. Was it because they had a striking resemblance or was Pastor Patterson really looking at me the same way? The sanctuary was full, but the gleam in her eye and the sideways smile showing only when she looked my way had me convinced she had a message just for me that went beyond the impassioned words shared with the church.

Every time her gaze passed over me, it was as if she was undressing me with her eyes. I decided it was not the resemblance to London. She wanted me.

By the third time it happened, I was seriously turned on. I couldn't believe I had a hard-on in church, albeit brought on by the finest pastor I'd ever known.

It seemed no one else had noticed our dancing glances or my current situation, but I removed my suit coat and placed it across my lap just in case.

As she made her way back across the stage, pinning me with her eyes once more, it became apparent I'd made the right choice with my coat. I gave up on the sermon, allowing my mind to drift as I thought about taking her back to my apartment for Sunday afternoon lovemaking.

Since I was pretty sure my thoughts were written all over my face, as soon as the service ended, I quickly headed for the exit. Only just through the sanctuary doors, Sarah Jacobs, my church stalker, stopped me.

"Hey," I said, surprised at her sudden appearance. "How are you?"

"Why haven't you returned any of my calls, Todd?"

"Um, I've been busy on a really difficult task," I lied, trying to avoid the awkward conversation she clearly was set on having.

"Busy doing what 'task' exactly?" She set her hands on her hips and stared into my eyes.

"Work, of course," I lied again. "I'm swamped with cases."

"Is that so?" she questioned, her voice laced with doubt. She didn't believe me. Hell, I didn't believe myself, but I found myself continuing the lies.

"Yeah, something like that," I responded hurriedly. "Listen, I really have to go."

"Not until you agree to have dinner with me," she demanded, throwing her arms around my neck. "And I don't care who in this church knows either."

Surely the middle of the church lobby wasn't the place for us to talk about this. Just then, Pastor Patterson's voice came from around the corner. The last thing I needed was for her to find Sarah all over me. I panicked and did the first thing I could think of to get Sarah off me.

"Okay," I quickly agreed. "When and where?"

"Tonight, at my place." She kissed me hard, slipping her tongue inside my mouth. "I'll text you my address."

As soon as Sarah removed her arms from around my neck, the sanctuary doors clicked open. Pastor Patterson appeared moments later surrounded by a host of parishioners.

That was a close one, I thought, looking toward the clustered group. Just then, Sarah indiscreetly pinched me on the ass, hard enough to make me jump.

"Are you okay, Todd?" she chuckled, apparently oblivious to my diverted attention.

"Yeah, I'm good," I said, feeling as if everyone in the lobby could sense my embarrassment. Just when I didn't think things could get any worse, Mr. Chandler walked through the doors, glanced my way and frowned, clearly not happy to see me. He sidled over to Sarah who was busy running her tongue over her lips, staring me down.

"I thought he was gone," he whispered loudly. Sarah ignored him.

"Todd," Pastor Patterson tapped me on the shoulder. "Can I have a word with you?"

"Of course," I responded enthusiastically as Sarah and Mr. Chandler looked on. Their expressions were almost comical.

"In private," she announced. I gladly followed her out of the lobby.

Chapter 21

MOMENTS LATER, WE were standing in the middle of the church parking lot, hand in hand. Without speaking, we both stepped closer and leaned in. The warmth of her body heat was emanating, radiating toward me as I breathed in her sweet scent. She held my eyes, my heart rate ratcheting up. Surely it was thudding loud enough for her to hear.

"Is everything okay?" I asked, sex on my mind.

"Everything is perfect." She squeezed my hands a little tighter. "Do you have any plans tonight?"

"The only plans I want to have tonight are with you, Pastor."

"Do you even know my first name, Todd?" she laughed.

"Yeah." I smiled. "It's Chloe."

"I see someone has been doing his homework," she teased, her eyes dancing with mine.

"Yeah," I said with a goofy smile. "I overheard your girl Angie calling you Chloe the other day at the hair salon."

"I'm glad you had a chance to meet them and doubly glad you came back to the church."

As a weighted silence fell between us, it was time for me to take charge and do what I had wanted to do all morning. I pulled her closer to me and leaned in.

Before I could make my move, she leaned back slightly, still grasping my hands tightly. "I like you, Todd," she sighed. "You're a great guy, but I have something very important to share with you."

"I like you too, Pastor," I said. "I feel the same way."

She just smiled.

As I continued to match her gaze, it seemed the light in her eyes mirrored the hope in my soul. I was exposed and vulnerable but somehow, also grateful for not needing to hide in her presence.

"I was right about you," she confided, tracing the side of my face with a perfectly manicured finger. "You're such a great guy."

As she dropped her hand from my face, the church doors opened to release the crowd of churchgoers. With a sigh, I glanced over, our moment broken. Sarah and Mr. Chandler were heading straight for me. The look on Mr. Chandler's face told me I was in for another tongue-lashing. I quickly slipped my hand into my pocket to grab my keys.

"I'll call you later!" I called to the pastor, turning and making a beeline for my car.

"Todd," Mr. Chandler called out. "We need to talk, son." Sarah was right behind him.

My car was still too far away. Sweat beads were forming on my forehead as the two of them closed in. Could Sarah have told Mr. Chandler that I'd agreed to have dinner with her?

And what about our lunch date and the kisses we'd shared? With these two on my back, my hopes of sealing the deal with Pastor Patterson seemed slim.

Glancing over my shoulder as I finally neared my car, I thought for a brief moment that I might make it out before my angry stalkers pinned me. Using the remote to unlock the car, I reached for the door handle. Someone grabbed at the back of my arm, like a pinch.

It was Blake.

"What are you doing here?" I was surprised, but happy to see him.

He had unwittingly just rescued me from being persecuted by Sarah and Mr. Chandler, neither of whom would want to pick a fight with me in front of him.

"What's up, TB?" He smiled at me as if he had just won the lottery. "You look like you've seen a ghost!"

"You have no idea," I said, watching over his shoulder as Sarah and Mr. Chandler turned and headed back inside the church. From their venomous looks, I owed Blake big time.

"Listen, TB." He wrapped his arm around my neck. "I have some exciting news to share."

"You made partner at the firm?" I asked.

"No, it's much bigger than that."

"You're starting your own firm?"

"No, TB." He laughed, facing me and grabbing me by the shoulders. "I'm getting married, man!"

"Married! What?" I said, shocked. I knew my boy well, and he wasn't the committing type. Every other week he was sleeping with another conquest; this had to be a joke. "Stop playing, man," I laughed. "You are the last person I'd ever expect to say, 'I do' to any woman."

"It's no joke," he assured me, a calm confidence radiating from him. "I'm in love. I'm in love for the first time in my life." He smiled beatifically. "She's amazing, bruh."

He sure sounded like a changed man. I decided to roll with it. "Okay, so who is this crazy-ass chick?" I asked, laughing again. "When do I get to meet her?"

"Let me introduce you." We headed back inside the church where a group of parishioners sat holding hands in a circle. Mr. Chandler and Sarah spotted us as soon as we entered the sanctuary and they dashed forward.

"Congratulations, brother!" they rang out in unison.

"I am so happy for you," Sarah said, her face in a wide smile.

She embraced Blake, peering over his shoulder to stick her tongue out at me.

"You are a very blessed man, Brother Harden." Mr. Chandler shook his hand, frowning at me.

"Thank you." He grinned.

As we made our way through the crowd, Blake beamed and pulled up short. It appeared we'd reached the lucky girl. "Honey, I would like to introduce you to my best friend, TB."

The woman in front of us turned around and my heart dropped.

"Pastor?" I croaked out. I glanced at Blake. "Pastor Patterson is your fiancée?"

"Yes, sir," he replied, slipping his hands into hers and planting a sweet kiss on her temple. The room seemed to be spinning in slow motion. Surely I was dreaming, and this was nothing but a terrible nightmare. Any moment, they would reveal it was all some horrible joke.

But as I stood there waiting, nothing changed. It was what it was. A nightmare. Blake still held Pastor Patterson's hands as she stared at me. The shock on her face mirrored my own.

"I didn't know you and Todd were friends," she finally said, glancing at him, nervous.

"Yeah, this is TB," he said. "But his slave name is Todd Banks."

Suddenly, a massive wave of disappointment came rolling through me. Staring at the obvious evidence of Blake's happiness, all the losses I'd experienced seemed to hit me simultaneously.

My thoughts spiraled back to my missed connection with London, who maybe could have made me as happy as Blake now seemed to be. But no matter how often my mind replayed our conversation on the train, I'd lost her. Not long after, I'd buried my father and been handed the bomb about my twin on the same day. Even Khalil's and my ill-fated rendezvous had been a failure and worse, it had left Henry badly injured.

Now, my best friend was engaged to marry the woman I wanted and who, until mere moments earlier, I had thought wanted me too.

The blows just kept coming.

It seemed grossly unfair to have been repeatedly betrayed by the people who claimed to care for me. This hell was my childhood all over again. No matter what Dr. Madison Perry said, the world was against me. Seeking escape, I spun around to leave, only to find myself face-to-face with Sarah, still eyeing me as if I was her favorite meal.

I spun back around. She was the last thing I needed right now.

With no way out, I sucked it up and plastered a broad, fake smile on my face. "Congratulations. I'm happy for the two of you."

"Thanks, TB. You will be my best man, right?" Blake offered.

Pastor Patterson's eyes met mine as I stood there motionless for a moment. "Of course," I recovered, shooting him a half smile. "I got you. Wouldn't miss it for the world."

My eyes were stinging. He would have thought it was emotion for their happiness. It was anything but. My heart was hurting. How much more of this heartache would God send to me?

"My man," he said, embracing me, slapping my back.

As more church members wandered over to offer their support and congratulations, I allowed the crowd to swallow me up. Backing quietly toward the exit, I mourned my losses with a heavy heart. Before pushing open the sanctuary doors, I risked a quick glance back over my shoulder. The pastor was staring at me, her eyes sad and round.

"I'm sorry," she mouthed silently. Instead of responding, I escaped through the double doors and moments later, found myself safely back inside my car. I took one final, long look at the church before lighting up a cigar and pulling out of the parking lot.

Chapter 22

HOW COULD I have been so blind? I pounded my fist against the steering wheel as I drove away from the church, trying to get my head around the situation. *Shake it off, Todd,* the voice inside my head said, pulling up to the local convenience store. I would drown my sorrows with a six-pack of Corona; numbing the craziness of my life had to be better than wallowing in it.

As I pulled into an open parking spot, the tires screeching slightly in my dazed state, it finally dawned on me why Blake had been so unexpectedly upset during our evening a while back at the Violet Lounge. I remembered it well since it had been the same day I'd received the call from my mother, saying that my father had passed away. His accusations about me sleeping with the pastor had seemed hypocritical at the time, especially coming from a known playboy like Blake.

Now that they were engaged, his motivations were abundantly clear.

But why hadn't he been man enough to tell me he had feelings for her then?

Or that he was involved with her romantically and on a serious level, too?

Instead, he'd laughed off our conversation and had hit the dance floor with some random hottie who'd happened to flash him a smile. And why had Pastor Patterson, a pastor and supposedly a person of great moral character, led me on? I ground my teeth, feeling as if I was missing something, unable to figure it out—but the six-pack would clear me of those thoughts.

I took a deep breath and pushed open the heavy glass door, stepping inside.

"Attorney Banks!" My Pakistani nemesis strode from behind the counter and greeted me with his customary slap to the back of the neck. "You arrest any bad guys today?" he asked in his heavily accented English. "How many you arrest? Many, huh?"

I wasn't in the mood for our usual verbal sparring. "For the one-hundredth time," I gritted, shrugging out of his grip, "I'm not a police officer. I'm an attorney."

He ignored me. "Many, many bad people in America," he complained, walking back behind the counter as I made my way to the coolers at the back of the store. "I really hate this country," he added. "It's evil. And it only gets worse, Attorney Banks. Only worse."

You have to be kidding me, I thought, dropping my six-pack on the counter, waiting for him to scan it before thrusting my Gold American Express card into the reader. "If you believe this country is so evil, why are you still here?" I was sick and tired of his America-bashing sessions. "You can always take your ungrateful ass back to your own country."

Bagging my purchase, he peered up at me and smiled crookedly. "Your ancestors came here to this country on slave ships, am I right?"

There was no winning with this guy. I wanted to punch him square in the face, but it would only keep me from my impending pity party. Instead, I roughly yanked my credit card from the reader, grabbed the plastic bag from the counter and walked out.

Before I could reach my car, his broken accent was calling out.

"Have a great night, Attorney Banks." He waved, smiling broadly. "And don't forget to arrest some more bad guys tomorrow. You stop this country from going more downhill."

Chapter 23

AS I SLIPPED MY key inside the door and entered my apartment, the weight of the world rested squarely on my shoulders. It had been an emotionally draining day, still offering no real answers. Popping open a Corona, I plopped myself down on the living room couch, kicking my feet up on the coffee table in front of me. Would my continued romantic misses—I tallied them up, being sure to include both London and Pastor Patterson—yet prove to be some sadistic ploy against me. Or had I somehow picked up a curse? It sure felt like it, also as if I was fighting God for a chance to play in the big leagues… and failing miserably.

I sighed and chugged down my beer, anticipating the escape my imminent buzz would bring.

Soon, I was pulling out my second Corona, flipping through the TV channels, not really paying attention. Suddenly, my phone began to ring. I definitely wasn't in the mood to talk, so I ignored it, not even glancing at the screen to see who was calling. But as soon as the voicemail icon popped up at the top of the screen, I tapped it.

I raised the phone to my ear, curiosity getting the better of me.

"Todd. It's Khalil. Call me when you get this message."

What could Khalil want? I tapped back to retrieve his number from the caller ID. Glancing at the screen, there was no number. The fool had called from a private, blocked one, offering no way to get back in touch with him. Would he be sitting there seething, believing me ignorant?

Like I said—I was cursed. Tossing the phone on the couch beside me, I kicked back as I finished my second beer. Seconds later, the phone buzzed again.

Perhaps Khalil had realized he didn't leave his phone number. Either way, I'd just settled back down, so like the first time, I let it go to voicemail.

And again like the first time, I was too curious to ignore the notification and lifted the phone to my ear. "Todd." My eyes widened as a woman's voice reached me this time. "It's Chloe. We need to talk. Please call me. I miss you. Things should never have happened that way."

"What the…" This was totally unexpected. What could she possibly want to talk about? I tapped back through the screen again and discovered that, unlike Khalil, she'd called from a listed number, so her digits were right there in front of me. I could feel my heart thumping violently. *Should I call her back? Ignore her?*

It didn't seem as though we had much to cover. It was what it was; she belonged to another man, my buddy Blake. It was hardly his fault, was it?

It was all to do with me, just my crap life with its equally crappy luck. But in light of her engagement to Blake, I didn't know what to do. How could I continue being friends with them both? But at the same time, I was not for letting go of Blake. Hell, we'd known each other for so long. What sort of friend let a woman come between us? *So, make it good. Just call her,* a little voice said. I grabbed the phone and hit the call button to redial her, then quickly hung up.

I can't. What's the point? There was nothing to pursue anymore. It was done. I was done.

As I paced the living room frantically with the phone in my hand, my blood pressure rose again, and I dialed her number a second time, wanting to hear her apologize, grovel and cry.

What kind of a game had she been playing with us both? Because it wasn't just me, was it? Blake's future was at stake, and I could have bedded this woman, could really have screwed up big time. When was she going to tell me about her and my boy Blake?

She had a lot of explaining to do, so maybe there were a few things we needed to cover.

You can't do this! I thought, hanging up again as the first ring trilled. "Think Todd, think!" I clamored aloud nervously. No answer was forthcoming, and in a fit of pique and disappointment in my incapable self, I dropped the phone onto the coffee table and plopped back down on the living room couch, staring at that wretched object. My adrenaline was still pumping.

I nearly had a heart attack when, less than two minutes later, the phone shrilled a third time.

I beelined toward it, hovering. A number popped up, unrecognizable. Yet again, it went to voicemail. My fingers were gripping the edge of the table, waiting for the voicemail notification.

Gingerly, the phone was brought to my ear once more.

"Hey baby, it's Sarah."

"Oh no," I sighed.

"I hope we're still on for dinner tonight. Call me. Ciao."

Things were spiraling out of control. So much crap had hit the fan that if I didn't get a hold of myself, I was going to lose my mind. Taking a deep breath, I decided enough was enough. It was time to corral this situation and get things straight.

I picked up the phone once more and punched in Sarah's number. It rang three times before her voice came onto the line.

"Hey, baby," she answered excitedly. "Are we still on for dinner?"

"Listen, Sarah," I said, popping open another beer and chugging it down in seconds. "I think you are an amazing woman, but I'm not the one for you. I will not be having dinner with you tonight or any night." There, I'd said it.

"What, why?" she screamed. "You are a low-life son of a whore. Don't ever call me again!" She hung up before I could say anything. I shrugged, relieved that conversation was over.

Next on the list was Chloe. This one would require another beer and a joint. I grabbed both, then nervously dialed her number. I bounced my foot as I waited for it to ring, my emotions barely in check.

"Todd?" Chloe's voice called out.

"Yeah," I responded, adding false toughness to my tone. "What do you want to talk about?"

"I'm so sorry about today." Her voice trembled. "I truly had no idea you and Blake were friends."

I didn't say a word, letting her apology hang in the air.

The silence dragged on for a few moments before her next declaration.

"I'm in love with you, Todd," she confessed. "I fell in love with you the moment I laid eyes on you."

This was too much. "But what about Blake?" I resounded.

"I know," she shot back. "I don't know what I was thinking when I accepted his proposal. We were out having dinner when he dropped to one knee and asked me to marry him. Before I could say no, I said yes. I'm so sorry, Todd. Please forgive me."

"Come on, Chloe," I said with an attitude. "How can you say you love me when you are engaged to my best friend? This isn't right."

"I know it isn't and I don't know how this mess happened," she blurted in frustration. "None of this is making any sense to me either."

Another moment of silence fell. Then she asked, "Are you saying that you don't love me, Todd? We're kindred spirits; I know you feel it too. You're my soulmate."

"I'm not your soulmate," I barked. "Apparently, your future husband and my best friend is."

"I made a huge mistake by agreeing to be his wife," she retorted. "I know that you love me. I could see it in your eyes today as we stood in the parking lot. I promise you, I will fix this."

I couldn't deny it; she was right. Feelings for her were burning in me, but how could I betray Blake? Despite his playboy antics, he didn't deserve it, especially from his best friend.

I couldn't just sit back and let things unravel like that. "I'm sorry, Chloe," I said in a constrained voice, trying to keep my emotions from coming through. "I cannot be with you."

"Please don't say that! My heart belongs to you and only you," she cried.

Before I could respond, our call was interrupted by a loud banging on my front door. "Hold on," I told Chloe, heading toward to the door to answer it. "Who's knocking?" I woofed.

"It's Blake, TB! Open up."

Chapter 24

DAMN! WORST TIMING ever! "Blake?" I called back. "Give me a second to put some clothes on. I'll be right there, man."

This day could not get any worse, I thought as I went dashing into my room to end my call with Chloe. "Listen," I said hurriedly, tucking the phone against my shoulder, "I have to go."

"Why?" she asked. "What's wrong?"

"Um," I said nervously. "I don't know how to say this, but your fiancé is at my front door."

"What?" she screeched. "Blake is there now?"

"Yes," I said in a frustrated tone. "I have to go."

"Put him on the phone," she insisted. "I am going to tell him all about us."

"About us?" I said with an attitude. "There is no us."

"Open the damn door, TB, or I'm going to let myself in!" Blake banged louder. "And you better not have one of those fine church women up in there either."

"If you won't put him on the phone," Chloe threatened, "I have no choice but to drive over there to tell him myself." With that, she hung up.

What the hell? Panic was kicking in. The last thing I needed was a lover's quarrel going down in my living room between my best friend and the woman who said she was in love with me. *What kind of pastor is she?* I fumed, hearing a key wrestling in the front door.

Seconds later, Blake walked in, obviously sloshed out of his mind.

"TB!" He drunkenly waved the spare key in the air, the one I'd given him. "Where is she?"

"Where is who?" I nervously peered out the living room window looking for Chloe's car.

Ignoring me, he grabbed a Corona from my half-empty six-pack and began searching my apartment like the police. "Where is she, TB?" he demanded again, stomping into my bedroom before suddenly face-planting on the bed.

"Get up, man," I yelled from the doorway, but it looked like the fool was out cold.

I dashed back and forth from the bedroom to the living room several times, trying to figure out my next move before Chloe arrived. My phone suddenly rang again, ripping me from my thoughts. I picked it up quickly this time. "Hello?" I whispered, dreading the answer.

"I'm almost there, Todd." She hung up before I could reply. Apparently, things were going down tonight whether I wanted them to or not.

I glanced toward my bedroom where Blake's feet were visibly dangling off the foot of my bed, then swiveled my gaze toward my front door where Chloe would soon be appearing.

Something was going to give tonight one way or the other and I had zero control over how things would go down. The gig was clearly up.

With no answer in sight, I did the one thing I told myself I would never do.

I sat down and I prayed.

"Lord, help me out of this mess." It was the only prayer I could think of. I repeated it several times over just to be sure, then heaved myself back to my feet. I didn't know how much a simple prayer like this could do, especially after so many years, but I had too much nervous energy to sit still any longer.

Glancing toward the door again, I had better find something to help take the edge off before it all hit the fan. A couple of Coronas still languished there in the six-pack I'd picked up earlier, but I shook my head. This night called for something stronger.

In the kitchen, a bottle of Jose Cuervo from the kitchen cabinet seemed to leap into my hands.

With the craziness about to ensue, being drunk was the only way to deal with it.

As I made my way back into the bedroom to grab my favorite Boston Red Sox shot glass, I discovered Blake now sprawled out on the floor in what looked like an incredibly uncomfortable position. Rolling my eyes, I stepped over him, strolling to the balcony to catch up with my dear old friend, tequila. One shot, then another. Before a third was possible, the phone rang. I just about made it back into the living room before the last ring. It was Chloe again.

"Todd, honey," she announced. "Is your boy still there?"

"He is." I tucked the phone against my shoulder as I stepped over him again and backed out onto the balcony. Peering down, I saw her exiting her car. "I'll be right down."

I hung up, then tiptoed back indoors to avoid awakening Blake. Amazingly, he was sitting up on the bed, vigorously rubbing at his eyes with the back of his hands.

"What the hell am I doing here, TB?" he greeted me, apparently having slept off his drunken stupor. He grabbed his car keys off the floor and stepped out onto the balcony. "Is this tequila for me?" he called, twisting off the cap and taking a swill straight from the bottle.

"It is now." I exhaled under my breath, reluctantly gathering myself to greet Chloe, leaving Blake with the bottle. As much as I hated the way things were about to go down, there was admittedly much relief the truth was finally coming out.

Before I could open the door, Blake's voice rang out again. "TB!"

You have got to be kidding me. I turned. "What?" I gritted out.

"Where is the toilet paper?"

"In the hall closet," I called back, slowly cracking open the door to reveal Chloe rocking a stylish gray, black and pink fitted jogging suit with matching shoes.

As usual, she looked as if she'd just stepped out of a fashion magazine.

"Hey, Chloe." I greeted her with a nervous smile.

He turned and smiled. "Seriously?"

"Yes," I said, peering through the glass window door to see Chloe heading our way. "Meet me in the living room so that we can put a plan together," I said and rushed out.

He turned to go. "Are you coming?" he asked, seeing that I wasn't behind him.

"I have to get something out of my car," I quickly lied.

"Hurry up!" he demanded. "It's time to celebrate again."

I opened the door and stepped out right in front of Chloe. Before I could say anything, she wrapped her arms around my neck and gently rubbed the side of my face.

"You smell amazing."

I was mesmerized by her and accepted the warmth and comfort of her embrace.

She pulled back and stared deep into my eyes. "Listen, I'm so sorry for bringing you into our mess," she apologized. "I only came back up to tell you I shouldn't have come here tonight. I will deal with this the way God wants me to deal with it."

"Thanks," I told her, relieved. "I appreciate you saying that."

"Please forgive me, Todd," she said, reaching up on her toes to kiss me on the cheek. It was nice, but in light of Blake's recent declaration, I would have preferred a kiss on the lips. "Call me, okay?" she asked.

She kissed my cheek a second time, then slipped on her baseball cap and headed back down the stairs toward her car. She slid behind the wheel and closed her car door, leaving me to heave out a giant breath unwittingly held onto for quite some time. Amazingly, the storm that had seemed so inevitable earlier in the evening had completely passed, without any damage at all.

For the first time all night, my face broke into a wide grin.

"Thank you, Jesus!" And I actually meant it.

Chapter 25

AS I RE-ENTERED my apartment, it was clear the tequila and Coronas had taken their toll. "What do you mean you're his twin brother?" Blake slurred drunkenly into my phone. Noticing me, he turned. "Who is Khalil?" he whispered loudly. "And why is he saying he's your twin brother?"

I grabbed the phone out of his hand. "Because he is. I'll explain it to you later."

"So, it's true?" Blake queried as I lifted the phone to my ear. He plopped down onto the couch and looked up at me, drunk and confused.

"What's up, Khalil? What do you want?" I added gruffly, putting on a hardcore front with Blake in the room. Besides, the whole incident with Henry still had me pissed.

"We need to talk," he barked. "You available tonight?"

I looked down at my wristwatch. 10:45 p.m., still relatively early. "Yeah, I guess. Meet me at the Violet Lounge in an hour," I said.

"See you there." He hung up before I could utter another word.

"TB." Blake grabbed the bottle of tequila from the table and chugged again. "What the hell is going on, man? I didn't know you had a twin."

"Neither did I." I grabbed my car keys from the coffee table and quickly exited the apartment with Blake weaving drunkenly behind me.

Chapter 26

ON OUR WAY to the violet lounge, I filled Blake in on the essentials. Once he'd heard the story, he began hammering me with questions.

"I cannot believe your family kept this secret from you for so long!" he ranted. Out of the corner of my eye, I saw him staring me down. "How does this make you feel? You cool? Nervous? Angry?"

"Listen," I said in a frustrated tone as we turned onto Interstate 93. "I don't really want to talk about it." This night had taken yet another crazy turn. All thoughts of talking to Blake about Chloe had flown out of the window with Khalil's call. *Why does he want to meet with me?* It wasn't like our first meeting had gone well, so why now? Why tonight?

As we pulled up, the line to get inside the Violet Lounge was draped around the corner. From the wide smile on his face, it was obvious Blake was a happy camper.

"It's Ladies' Night, T.B.!" he exclaimed, rolling the car window down. "Look at all of the fine honeys out tonight!" He stared at the parade of women dressed to kill, practically drooling.

"Calm down, player," I said. *Didn't take long to forget Chloe,* I thought sarcastically as we pulled into the parking garage, amazingly finding an empty parking spot on the first level.

Parking was always an issue at the Violet Lounge; scoring a prime spot was highly unusual, but I wasn't protesting. As we strolled toward the entrance, I wondered briefly whether my prayer from earlier might still be in effect. *Did God care enough to provide me with a sweet parking spot?* I shrugged to myself, grateful either way.

I was on a mission tonight and the sooner I caught up with Khalil, the better.

Since the owner of the lounge was a former client of mine, I always got VIP service. As Blake and I walked up, there too was my church stalker, Sarah, a ways back from the front of the line. She was chatting with a beautiful, brown-skinned woman with long black hair and killer curves.

"Hey, Todd," she called, spotting me and rushing forward.

She grabbed the back of my arm, pulling me toward her. "I'm going to forgive you for being so rude to me earlier tonight," she told me. "When did you start riding a motorcycle?" she asked, moving in closer to press her breasts against my arm as she inhaled deeply. "You smell amazing," she whispered, staring at me lustfully.

"I don't ride a motorcycle," I corrected her, glancing at Blake for help.

"Well, you must have a twin then," she declared. She nudged her friend who was eyeing me up and down. "Didn't I tell you he was fine?"

"He is that." Sarah's friend flashed a bright smile, revealing perfectly straight teeth. "Two for the price of one!" she laughed. With her eyes practically undressing me, Sarah began rubbing my shoulders aggressively. I quickly stepped back, disengaging from her grasp.

"Ladies," Blake chimed in, saving me from further embarrassment. "Would the two of you like to join us in the VIP room?"

He waved his gold VIP card in the air as if it were the winning Megabucks ticket.

"Hell yeah!" they shouted in unison.

"Follow me," he bolstered. I sighed, resigning myself to spending more time with my stalker. Hopefully, I could find Khalil quickly and get out of there before things got too bad.

As the four of us headed to the front of the line, Sarah sidled up, attaching herself to my arm again. Glancing over at Blake, she whispered, "Isn't he engaged to the pastor?"

Instead of lying, I just shrugged.

"Are you sure you don't own a motorcycle?" Sarah questioned a second time, slipping her hand into mine and pressing against my side seductively. Not waiting for my answer, she continued, "Do you like my outfit?" She smiled, changing gears.

She was wearing a fitted green tank dress with gold, ankle-strap stilettos.

"You look very nice," I said politely, making sure to keep my gaze on her eyes and not her cleavage.

"And this nicely wrapped package could have been all yours tonight." She pouted, staring at me with her ocean-blue eyes. "I don't know why you keep blowing me off."

"I'm just not ready," I evaded, recalling Chloe's declarations of love earlier in the evening. Did I love Chloe in return? I wasn't sure. Unexpectedly, my thoughts also jumped back to my rendezvous on the train with London. *That was forever ago, Todd!* I chastised myself, though her beautiful face remained in my mind. *Why are you still **thinking of her?***

She didn't show any interest in you. Didn't even give you her goddamn number.

Somehow, London continued to weave her way through my mind at least a few times a week, even though it had been ages since we'd crossed paths.

I shook my head quickly, trying to shift my thoughts.

When we reached the front of the line, Blake handed his VIP card to the bouncer. He gave us the once-over. "Didn't I just let you in?" he questioned me. "Where is your motorcycle helmet?"

"You must have me confused with someone else," I laughed, trying to keep things moving.

"There is a guy inside that I swear looks just like you," he said. "You twins or somethin'?"

He shook his head as he removed the velvet rope to allow the four of us in.

As we entered, Sarah finally released me so she and her girl-friend could hit the dance floor.

Khalil was sitting at the bar, sipping on a bottle of water. I strolled over, Blake close behind.

"Khalil," I made myself known. "This is my boy, Blake."

Blake took one look at Khalil and then looked over at me, rapidly shifting his gaze between the two of us several times. "No damn way," he shouted. "Am I seeing double?"

I ignored him.

"So, what do you want to talk about?" I asked Khalil, cutting straight to the point.

"Not in here," he replied. He reached down for his motorcycle jacket and helmet. "Let's take a walk outdoors."

"I'll be right back," I signaled to Blake, now blatantly ogling Sarah and her friend.

"Take your time, TB." He waved.

"Same ol' Blake," I whispered under my breath, following Khalil out of the Violet Lounge.

After a short walk to a nearby parking lot, Khalil stopped in front of what I presumed was his motorcycle. He spun around to face me. "Listen, man. I want to apologize for the way I acted when we met," he said, his voice hard. "Up until a few weeks ago, I didn't even know you existed. This is a lot for me to take in, but… Well, I'm willing to get to know you, to give it a try." He extended his right hand.

I eyed him for a moment, trying to gauge his sincerity. I shrugged. *What do I have to lose?* I thought. "Okay," I agreed, extending my hand in return. We shook on it.

"And I guess it's kind of messed up what happened to your friend at the warehouse. I thought someone was sneaking up on me," he stated with a hint of remorse without actually saying it.

"Well, I guess this is going to be a lot for you to take in too, but he's your brother too, our older brother, Henry," I expressed. "You nearly killed your own flesh and blood back there."

With a deep sigh of exasperation, Khalil said, "call me," and handed me a piece of paper with his phone number on it. I watched as he slipped on his motorcycle jacket and helmet.

He hopped onto his Kawasaki sports bike. Before he took off, he turned to me with a sharp look as if considering whether to say more.

After a short pause, he said, "Your boy Blake…he's a snake, right? Don't trust him." With that, he revved his bike as he kicked back the kickstand. Over the roar, didn't he shout out, "Peace, bruh!" Or was it merely my imagination? Seconds later, he was gone.

As I stood listening to the bike's engine disappearing out into the city, his final comment finally registered.

*****

I made my way back inside the club to find Blake still on the dance floor jamming with Sarah's girl to the hit song 'No Limit.' Catching my eye from across the room, he leaned down to say something to her before quickly heading my way.

"So, what happened?" he demanded, throwing his arm around my neck and leading me back toward the bar.

"Nothing," I said casually.

"Nothing," he scoffed. "You were gone for a while. That doesn't sound like nothing to me."

"Really," I promised as we reached the bar. "It was nothing."

"What did he say?" he pressed.

"Can I get a shot of Hennessy and a Corona?" I instructed the bartender.

"If we're boys, then you won't keep this from me," he continued.

"Fine," I barked back. "We decided to make an attempt at getting to know each other."

Apparently, it was the wrong answer. Blake grabbed my shot from the bar and threw it back.

"I don't know why you'd want to build a relationship with someone who is clearly a thug, regardless of any blood relationship. Doesn't make sense to me. I'm more of a brother to you than he'll ever be," he complained.

"Well." I ordered another shot, hoping I'd actually be able to enjoy this one myself. "I suppose time will tell. And you know it's got nothing to do with you and me. We're brothers too. There's nothing going to come between you and me."

Blake was uncharacteristically silent, staring off into space with that angry expression.

"What's wrong with you?" I asked. I took a sip of my Corona.

"Don't trust him, T.B.," he said, seething. "Your brother Khalil Gilliam's just bad news."

"How do you know his last name?" I asked suspiciously. I hadn't mentioned it all evening.

"Oh, um," he stuttered, "I saw it earlier on your phone when he called." He spun around and headed back onto the dance floor.

Chapter 27

I WAS CHILLING in the lobby at gold's gym, catching up on text messages, waiting for Blake to arrive. He finally strolled in, holding hands with the woman he'd met at the Violet Lounge.

"What's up, Blake?" I pulled him to the side and lowered my voice. "Isn't she the one who was out with Sarah last night?" I asked, inclining my head toward his gym date.

"Yes, sir." He beamed. "And she took very good care of your boy last night. I think she's a keeper, man."

"A keeper? You told me just yesterday you were a player who couldn't be tied down!"

"Sure, but look at her, man," he boasted, gesturing vaguely behind him at his new friend who was totally engrossed in her phone. "Five foot four, one hundred twenty-five pounds and built like Jennifer Lopez. And she's a smokin' mix of Asian and black."

As I glanced over his shoulder, I had to admit Blake was right. She was definitely a looker with a killer body to match. Still, I wasn't about to take his new love interest seriously. Last time we'd spoken, no woman was going to pin him down, and the time before, he'd been engaged.

As he rambled on about his latest conquest, my phone went off once, twice, three times. The dings continued: someone was serial texting me. Blake finally took notice.

"Who's blowing your phone up, TB? Sarah, isn't it?" he said and laughed.

"Nah, it's not Sarah," I answered honestly, scrolling through the new messages.

Given the roller coaster ride Blake had put me through yesterday, I decided spur of the moment, it was time for some payback. "It's Pastor Patterson!" I lied, grinning. "She wants to hook up later today to talk." Not waiting for his response, I turned and began walking toward the exercise mats for a pre-workout stretch.

"What?" he said through gritted teeth as he fell in to walk beside me. "What the hell does she want to talk to you about?" he asked sharply, trying to keep his voice down as his arm candy trailed behind us, still glued to her phone.

"I don't know, man." I shrugged nonchalantly.

"What the hell does she want to talk to him about?" he repeated, falling back a step to ask his latest bedmate. The repeat question obviously wasn't intended for me, but as I overheard, I smiled to myself. My little ploy was making waves.

Enjoying myself, I decided to take my lie a little further.

"Anyways," I continued, pretending I hadn't heard him as I settled myself onto an exercise mat and began stretching my hamstrings. "Now that the two of you are no longer engaged, would you have a problem if I asked her out?"

"Like on a date?" He stopped his own stretching to stare at me in the mirror in front of us.

"Yeah," I replied, keeping it casual as I switched it up and stretched out my quads. "Something like that."

"That's crazy," he barked as he turned to face me. "I haven't even told her the engagement is off. Hell, I still may go through with it!" he proclaimed.

"Really?" I replied coolly, raising my eyebrow. "Just last night, you told me you couldn't commit to just one woman.

And what about Sarah's friend?" I motioned to the hottie sitting on the floor behind him, still tapping away at her screen, oblivious to our conversation.

I was beginning to think her phone was surgically attached to her hands.

"I actually brought her here for you," he covered quickly. "I mean, you really need to get back into the game," he joked halfheartedly.

I rolled my eyes but didn't reply, deciding it was best to let it go. His attitude did make me wonder though. *What is it about him and Chloe?* I mused. *One minute he's celebrating being single, but as soon as I mention her name, he's ready to recommit? I don't get it and Chloe definitely deserves better.* As we finished our warm-up and headed over to hit the weights, I considered taking his punk ass down and demanding answers. But as much as I wanted to get to the bottom of things, getting physical wouldn't solve the problem.

Whatever Blake was hiding, he wasn't talking. So I channeled my energy into my workout. As I knocked out the first few reps, my head was beginning to clear.

*****

An hour later, I was pumped up and feeling good. Checking myself in the mirror, I followed behind Blake and his phone-obsessed chick, once again holding hands now that she'd finally managed to part herself from that wretched gadget of hers.

As we headed for the exit, I stepped up on his other side and leaned in. "I thought you brought her here for me," I reminded him.

He laughed as we walked through the doors, then turned to face me. "Nah, she isn't your type." He winked as the doors closed behind us. "Later, TB!" He waved. Seconds later, the two of them peeled out of the parking lot in his Porsche.

I shook my head, slipping into my own ride.

Chapter 28

BEFORE I COULD make it two blocks, my boy Blake was blowing up my phone already.

"What's up?" I pulled into the gas station, lowered the music and reached into the glove compartment for a cigar.

"Chloe just called," he blurted, his voice serious for once. "The engagement is off."

"So you decided to call it off even though earlier you said you might go through with it?" I asked, trying to keep it all straight.

Blake didn't answer, instead remaining uncharacteristically silent.

"Wait, you mean she told you the engagement was off?" I said as I fit the pieces together. My mind sped forward at the possible ramifications of this news.

"Yes," he snapped. "She dropped the bomb on me. She told me that she couldn't marry a man she didn't love and the only reason she agreed to my proposal was to save me from embarrassment in front of my family. I'm hurt, man."

"You literally just drove off with some other woman in your car, Blake. Besides, yesterday you told me you didn't want to marry her anyways."

"That was before you…" He stopped short mid-sentence.

"Before I what?" I pressed.

"It's not important, man." He sighed. "I'm the one who's just lost the love of my life. Chloe is really special." He sighed again.

Suddenly, I regretted my game from earlier. Blake seemed really beat up over the news. "I'm sorry, man," I offered sincerely, wallowing in a surge of guilt.

Here I was messing with him when I hadn't been honest either. Blake needed to know the truth and considering how long we'd been boys, it had to come from me.

"Listen, Blake." I cleared my throat, figuring now was as good a time to come clean as any. "I have something very important to tell you."

"What could be more important than what's going on in my world?" he moped, his voice conveying a hefty dose of self-pity.

I ignored his play for attention and took a deep breath.

"I am the..." I began. Before I could finish my sentence, another call beeped in. I glanced at the screen. Chloe! *Hell no.* I immediately second-guessed myself, unsure of whether or not to continue my conversation with Blake. But it just wasn't in me to ignore Chloe's call, so I went against my better judgment. "Hold on, Blake. I got another call coming in."

My heart pounded in my chest. At this rate, I'd be getting panic attacks.

"Make it quick," he said with an attitude.

"Will do." I clicked over. "Hello?"

"Hi, Todd. It's Chloe." The sweet sound of her voice cornered me. "Am I catching you at a bad time?"

"Not at all," I lied quickly. "What's up?"

"I just told Blake that the engagement is off." Her voice was shaking. "And it didn't go well. I feel like I just broke his heart, Todd."

"I know, well... Just... Just give me a second, all right? Blake is on the other line right now."

"Okay," she said. "I'll be waiting."

I put her on hold, but before I clicked over to Blake, I

paused. "God," I said, looking at the sky through my windshield. "Please tell me what to say." Saying it felt right, but this was the second time I had prayed in less than twenty-four hours.

What is happening to me? I shook my head to clear it, secretly hoping this prayer might be as effective as the last one.

I tapped my screen again. "Sorry about that, Blake, but I had to answer that."

"Who was it?" he demanded.

"It was Pastor Patterson," I confessed immediately. I was done with lying.

"What?" he yelped. "What did she want and why is she calling you?"

"She called to tell me that the engagement was off," I answered. "She's still on the other line. Let me hang up with her, okay?"

"No," he snapped. "Don't hang up."

"Why not?" I asked.

"Because I want to know what's really going on with the two of you."

"Okay," I said, more than ready to clear the air. "But in person, it will be better. Meet me at Metro Café in thirty minutes and I'll tell you everything?"

"I'm on my way."

After he hung up, I clicked back over to Chloe.

"I just hung up with Blake," I said, relieved this convoluted nightmare was about to come to an end. "He wants to know why you and I are so close. I can't lie to him anymore, Chloe. I'm meeting him at Metro Café in thirty minutes to tell him the truth about us."

"Okay but are you sure this is the right time? I just broke off our engagement."

Tell me something I didn't know already!

"I know you did, but yeah, I'm sure," I told her. I smiled, confident in my answer.

"Then, I'm on my way," she announced. "It's only right that he hears it from both of us. And there's no way I'd leave you on your own to tell him. It'd make me a bad person."

Chapter 29

I RELUCTANTLY STEPPED inside Metro Café. Blake and Chloe were already there, sitting at a window booth near the entrance, holding hands and looking like the perfect couple. I sighed.

This wasn't going to be easy. It wouldn't surprise me if Blake said they were back together.

"Good morning," greeted the hostess, a gorgeous, dark-skinned cutie with long dreadlocks and a bright smile. She gave me a once-over before her eyes locked on mine. "Will you be dining alone?" she asked, her smile widening.

"Not today," I said. "My friends are already here," I added, gesturing toward the window booth. I hoped 'friends' would still be accurate after I confessed everything.

"Great," she replied, grabbing a menu and a set of utensils neatly rolled up in a white paper napkin. "Follow me."

As we made our way through a maze of little tables toward the booth where Blake and Chloe waited, I glanced curiously at the other patrons, wondering who else would be in the room when I bared my soul. I noticed an Asian couple playing footsies under the table, gazing adoringly into one another's eyes. Their connection was incredibly intense, almost tangible.

This was how love should be. It wasn't a game, not something to take lightly.

Without warning, my mind jumped back to London's piercing stare, and I wondered if the others who'd been on the Red Line train to Cambridge the day we'd met had felt our connection as intensely as I felt this Asian couple's.

Though it had been nearly a year since our chance encounter, London still haunted my waking and sleeping dreams, popping unexpectedly into my mind at least once a week.

I couldn't understand why I still longed for a stranger, especially when I was moments away from confessing my love for a beautiful woman who not only knew me but had already expressed her love for me.

I wished I could stop thinking of London, but every time I remembered our first meeting, I wanted to see her again. *Why can't I just let her go?* I asked myself for the millionth time.

It was infuriating. I shook myself out of my reverie as we finally reached the table where Blake and Chloe waited. The hostess came by again, laying down the menu and silverware, seemingly oblivious to the mood in our small group. Whatever were the pre-requisites for getting hired as a waitress, they did not include sensitivity and tact. Blake stood quickly, turning to face me and staring me down as if we were boxers in the ring before a championship bout.

On edge thanks to my errant thoughts moments earlier as well as the heavy subject we were all here to discuss, this rendezvous could go sideways in a second.

Matching his gaze, I felt myself clenching my fists. If I had to, I'd knock his teeth down his throat. But instead of a swing, Blake flashed me a gigantic smile.

"It's about time," he joked as he threw his arm around my neck and squeezed. "At this rate, you'll be late for your own funeral." He and Chloe laughed in unison.

Rather than diffusing the tense situation, their friendly camaraderie set me even more on edge.

"Your server will be with you in a moment," the hostess chirped as Blake resumed his seat next to Chloe. I wanted to scream, *who gives a crap about the server? Just leave us in peace!*

"Hi, Todd," Chloe murmured as I took my seat as well. "It's great to see you."

"You too," I returned, peering over at Blake to get his take on her comments, but his face was impassive. As silence fell and then dragged on, the moment had arrived for me to come clean. My gut twisted. I didn't want to break the ice, so instead clammed up, feeling stupid.

Moments later, my discomfort was temporarily relieved as a slender-built woman with curly red hair and freckles appeared at our table. *Well, thank God for a server after all.*

"Good morning," she greeted us warmly. "My name is Quinn, and I will be your server today. Can I start you off with something to drink?"

"Very nice to meet you, Quinn," Chloe chimed, resting her elbows on the table. "I think I will have your Chai tea and a small glass of water with a lemon on the side."

She glanced over at Blake who was still staring me down.

He answered without looking her way.

"I will have a large, sweet tea and a glass of water without the lemon."

"And for you, sir?" she asked me.

"Coffee and water will be fine," I said, poker-faced.

"Thank you." She slipped her pen and pad into her apron pocket. "I'll be right back with your drinks."

With our server gone, Chloe and Blake mulled over their menus.

On edge as I was, their chatter about what to order irked me, and the only way to alleviate my discomfort was to break my silence. I covertly wiped my sweaty palms on the sides of my gym shorts, took a deep breath and made my move.

"So, what do you want to know?" I rushed out, looking across the table at Blake.

"Whatever you are ready to tell me," he countered, inching forward in his seat and leaning closer, staring at me.

Before I could reply, Chloe nudged Blake hard with her elbow. Breaking his stare, he met her eyes briefly. The two of them started to laugh.

"What's so funny?" I spat out, finding little humor in the situation.

"Calm down, playboy," Blake smiled. "Chloe told me the whole story."

"Oh yeah? And what story is that?" I asked with a raised eyebrow. Judging by the way Blake and Chloe were behaving, it seemed there were more lies at work here than just my own. "What story are you talking about?" I asked again, louder this time.

"I was wrong for trying to keep the two of you apart," Blake said. He extended his hand. "Forgive me, TB."

"Keeping us apart?" I questioned, ignoring his hand. "I don't understand. What are you talking about?"

"That night at the Violet Lounge when I thought you'd slept with Chloe upset the hell out of me," he confessed.

I'd figured that much out myself. "I know it did. I was there. Stop talking in riddles!"

My fist hammered on the tabletop, making a number of restaurant patrons turn curiously toward us. I dropped my hand to my lap, lowering my voice.

"Tell me what's really going on here. I deserve to know."

Blake glanced at Chloe again before answering.

She nodded slightly, encouraging him. "All right, TB, here it is. The truth is, Chloe and I are old childhood friends. We grew up together; I've known her since we were ten years old," he declared. I sat, shock frozen on my face at his pronouncement. Before I could pull it together, Blake continued. "There's something else you should know too."

With perfect timing as usual, the server returned with a tray full of drinks. Setting them down, she pulled out her notepad. "Are you all ready to order?"

"Not quite," I said in a frustrated tone.

"All right, I'll give you a few more minutes."

She smiled and moved on to check on her next table.

"Listen, Todd," Chloe said gently, reaching across the table to touch the back of my hand. In other circumstances, her gesture might have calmed me, but with the news of their long-standing friendship hanging between us, I hardly registered the skin-to-skin contact.

She looked over at Blake. "Should I tell him?" she asked. He smiled, then nodded at her as I stared them both down, bouncing my leg under the table impatiently.

"Look, whatever it is, just spit it out," I said roughly. I was probably too loud again, but needed answers, and didn't care who else heard.

"Okay," Chloe said, finally picking up on my anxiety. "Ever since we were kids, our parents wanted us to get married," she rushed. "Now, given your friendship, you probably know Blake's mother's in hospice with terminal cancer. Since she began hospice, she's repeatedly stated that her dying wish is to see the two of us get married. We just couldn't break her heart by saying no, not while she is on her deathbed. So... when Blake asked me in front of his mother and other family members, I said yes. It was only supposed to be for her, but with other family members in the room, the news of our engagement spread like a wildfire."

Nodding, Blake took over the story.

"By the time we realized what was happening, it was already done, and we couldn't break Mom's heart by calling it off, not when she was so excited about it. When I found out that night at the Violet Lounge that you were interested in Chloe, I started to get angry, worried that you would ruin the whole charade and destroy my mother's last moments of happiness if it got out that something was going on between the two of you."

I slowly leaned back against the plastic padding of the booth, trying to process everything they'd just shared. I was aware Blake's mom was in hospice and they had a close relationship. I could certainly understand not wanting to let down a terminally ill parent.

Still, I didn't understand how these two people, who both knew me well, could have kept so much from me. They had both betrayed me. "But what about the truth?" I blurted, leaning forward in my seat again. I stared at Blake.

"We're boys like you always say. How could you keep so much from me?" I shifted my eyes to Chloe. "And you, you're a pastor! Isn't it your purpose and mission to spread love and truth?"

Her eyes welled with tears at my accusations. "Yes," she said simply. "I'm so sorry for keeping you in the dark, Todd," she apologized, searching my eyes. "It was wrong of us to keep this from you. I hope you can forgive me," she pleaded.

"I'm sorry too, man," Blake added remorsefully.

I leaned back again. Their apologies seemed sincere enough, but I'd been kept in the dark for so long that I wanted to hold their lies against them. I felt justified. But as upset as I was at their deceit, the truth was, I hadn't been honest with them either. Maybe if I had, everything would have come out sooner and none of us would be in this crazy situation. Then again, I wasn't sure I wanted everything to come out. What about the feelings I still secretly harbored for London?

As much as I cared for Chloe, I definitely wasn't ready to share my inexplicable fixation. I still didn't understand that one myself.

But since Blake and Chloe had just come clean, I could hardly stay angry with them, especially now that I understood their motive for keeping secrets. But that didn't mean I had to bare my soul completely. I'd forgive them—but I'd be keeping news of London to myself.

I pulled my gaze from my lap up to meet their worried faces. Releasing a big sigh, I smiled at them both. "It's cool," I told them. "I don't like lies but do understand why you both did what you did. I forgive you," I said, watching their tense expressions relax as I spoke.

"Thank you, Todd," said Chloe with a smile.

Blake nodded his agreement.

"Well, thanks for telling me the truth." I smiled back and looked at them expectantly. "So… what do we do now?"

Chapter 30

"THE TWO OF YOU should tie the knot!" Blake rang with excitement, my gaze fixated on him with suspicion. Was this his way of messing with me because he was still upset that I had feelings for his old friend? Or did he just want to get a rise out of me while he had me cornered?

"Get married?" I tried laughing it off. "Stop joking. What about your mom's dying wishes? Your whole family thinks you're the ones getting married, not me."

"Of course, we have some explaining to do," he said. "But why not?" His expression was serious as he met Chloe's eyes.

This was crazy. I had to put a stop to his shenanigans before everyone in the restaurant started tossing bird seed our way. "Because we hardly know each other," I said straightforwardly, confident my logic would stop him in his tracks.

"I'm not saying the two of you need to get married *today*," he chuckled back. "But I'm thinking that six months should be a long enough engagement, wouldn't you say?"

Suddenly, everything began to move in slow motion as I realized Blake was dead serious. He actually thought I should marry Chloe, apparently six short months from now. But less than three hours earlier, he had been engaged to her. Now he was pawning her off like an old piece of jewelry. How could he think this was a good idea? Hell no, I told myself firmly, turning toward Chloe for support. Surely I wasn't the only one who thought this was happening way too fast.

She didn't meet my eyes, though, staring down at her empty ring finger, smiling.

"Well, I do love you, Todd," she stated, raising her gaze to lock eyes with me. She reached across the table to entwine her fingers with mine.

I opened my mouth, then closed it without saying anything. *The two of you are crazy as hell!* I thought, shifting my stare between them. Not wanting to offend Chloe, instead of reacting,

I kept my mouth shut as my thoughts whirled. Yes, I loved her, but as for marriage…? Without warning, London popped into my mind yet again.

Was I ready to give up on whatever it was I still felt for her? What if our paths led us to one another again? What if the stars did align in our favor after all?

Think Todd, think! A small voice was nudging me. *London's long gone,* a louder voice rang, and *Chloe's the next best thing. Don't let her out of your grasp! London wasn't ever in your life!*

With the pressure mounting, I felt trapped.

"So, what do you think, TB?" Blake repeated, shooting me a loaded stare.

"It's a little soon to be thinking about tying the knot, especially when the two of you are still engaged, don't you think?" I evaded.

"We just called it off," he pressed. "Are you saying that Chloe isn't marriage material?"

"I never said that," I replied gruffly. "Seriously though, what about your mom, Blake? A moment ago, you made it sound like it would break her heart if you two didn't say 'I do.' You don't want to stress her with this news, do you?"

I hated to play the sick parent card, but desperately needed to get out of this mess.

A wave of pain crossed Blake's face. "Unfortunately, Mom took a turn for the worse shortly after I popped the question. She's too far gone to comprehend it even if we told her. Go ahead TB. It's fine," Blake stated sadly, though he gave me a small half-smile.

My back was up against the wall, having thrown every excuse I could think of at them, but I was still in the hot seat, unready to commit, but unable to say no. For some reason, that word wouldn't leave my lips. My heart pounded against my ribcage as they both stared.

This must have been how they'd felt when Blake's mom insisted they get married.

As the minutes dragged, Blake decided to take my silence as an answer.

"Well, it's a done deal then, right?" he egged.

Some friend, I thought viciously, mean-mugging him. He smiled back at me. I was losing this game big time. Seeking reprieve, I glanced over at Chloe.

"I would marry you tomorrow if you asked me," she voiced as she met my eyes. "I'm in love with you, Todd. And I'd love to spend my life with you."

Checkmate, I thought, knowing there was only one reply to a comment like that. With a half-hearted smile, I leaned back and looked across the table at the two of them. "Yeah," I said in a low voice, shoving down my lingering thoughts of London. "I'm cool with it."

Chapter 31

LESS THAN THREE months later, Chloe and I were officially engaged, deeply immersed in the throes of wedding planning. With Blake's encouragement, I'd already basically proposed back at the diner. Chloe was expecting a ring, so there had seemed no point in delaying the inevitable.

News about our impending nuptials spread rapidly thanks to Blake and his big mouth. He made sure everyone in the church knew within a week of me officially popping the question.

Much to my surprise, the church members were very understanding of Chloe's announcement that her engagement with Blake was off and that we were the couple tying the knot instead.

No one would ever question their pastor. The Lord worked in mysterious ways; that was the widespread proclamation in the church. Her congregation genuinely wanted the best for her, and once she confirmed that meant being with me and not Blake, they accepted it easily.

Everyone seemed truly happy for us—with one glaring exception. In light of our announcement, Sarah had cut me off completely. It was not a loss.

She'd even left the church. In our last conversation, she'd informed me I had ruined her faith to the point where she would never set foot inside the church again.

I wanted to feel badly about her proclamation, but mostly, felt relieved about not having to cross paths with her anymore.

Even Mr. Chandler had finally warmed up to me after realizing I would be second-in-charge at the church as soon as Chloe and I were married.

I'd be king of the hill as soon as the deed was done, and I was looking forward to the power trip my new position would give me. There seemed to be no examples to guide me on how married couples in a church operated, but how hard could it be up there at the top?

I was confident of figuring it out once secure in my new role.

Meanwhile, over the past few months, Khalil and I had grown closer. Though I still didn't know much about his day-to-day life, we'd managed to build a surprisingly strong, brotherly relationship. At my request, he had even agreed to meet Mom and our other siblings.

Unfortunately, it had been short-lived, however. My family didn't trust him because of his assault on Henry and he felt they'd all betrayed him. They had known about him, but never reached out or informed me of his existence. Still, I was grateful to have him in my life now.

Overall, life was finally beginning to look up for me. As I sat on my balcony one Saturday morning, sipping a Corona and enjoying yet another Black & Mild, I had to admit the whole engagement thing was turning out better than I'd thought. Though I'd initially felt swept along by the current, all the pieces seemed to be falling into place on their own these days.

My doubts about getting married still lingered at the back of my mind, but rather than fight the tide, I'd just keep rolling with it.

And so I did—at least until the night of my rehearsal dinner just a few months later.

Chapter 32

IT WAS JUST a few minutes before our rehearsal celebration was officially supposed to start. Blake, Chloe and I were chatting inside the ballroom at the luxurious Ritz Carlton hotel with Chloe's childhood friend, Monica Jones, a Kerry Washington look-alike. Blake had just tipped back a shot of Hennessy when Khalil strolled into the ballroom, dressed in black from head-to-toe.

"I didn't know you invited him," Blake accused in a loud whisper, plunking his shot glass on the table with unnecessary force.

"You're tripping," I replied with an attitude as I rose to meet Khalil. "He's my brother. Of course, I invited him. It'd be un-Christian not to, don't you think?" Knowing how Blake felt about Khalil, I hadn't been forthcoming about our increasingly close relationship, but figured he could at least appreciate me wanting my twin brother present for such a big occasion.

After all, life had cruelly kept us apart for so long. It was time to make up for the past.

Blake stood up as well. "I'm not sure I'll ever accept a thug like him," he continued, though he began walking beside me. We headed toward Khalil, who was scanning the room from the doorway, obviously in search of me. "He's bad news, TB. I just don't trust him."

"Listen," I said, thinking back to the numerous times Blake had deceived me over the years. "You're the one who told me that no one is without sin and that we are all saved by grace. Maybe you need to cut him some slack."

"Yeah, but that only applies to followers of Christ," he stated arrogantly. "And we both know that felon isn't a Christian."

"Maybe not, but it does apply to you, right?" I laughed. "Based on your logic, a man who sleeps with every woman in the church deserves grace, but my brother doesn't? You are a hypocrite, my friend, and it's one of the reasons I don't put much stock in attending church."

"Whatever, man." Blake shrugged.

"I'm glad you could make it," I told Khalil, greeting him with a brotherly hug.

"Of course." He peered over my shoulder and shot Blake a murderous glare. "I wouldn't have missed it for anything."

"What's up with your drive-by outfit?" I joked. Everyone at the rehearsal dinner was dressed in their Sunday best, but not Khalil. I couldn't imagine him in a suit and tie anyway.

But I admired him for not trying to fit in.

"Just being me, bruh."

"I like that."

"Is there an open bar?" he asked, scanning the ballroom.

"There is," I replied as I threw my arm around his neck. "But first, let me introduce you to a few people." I led him back to the table where Chloe and Monica were still chatting animatedly.

"Chloe," I called. Her head swiveled in my direction as we neared. "This is my brother, Khalil," I introduced.

"Holy mother," she gasped, her eyes darting back and forth from Khalil's face to mine.

"I tried to tell you that we were identical," I laughed. "Khalil, this is my fiancée, Chloe."

"Nice to meet you, Chloe." He extended his right hand as he looked her up and down. "My brother has told me all about you. I trust you will take very good care of him, right?"

"Of course." She shifted her eyes back toward me. "I love Todd."

"So you are the bad twin, huh?" Monica chimed in. Khalil didn't even acknowledge the comment, looking straight through Monica as if she were invisible.

"What about that drink?" he asked me a second time.

"I didn't know he had a twin," Monica whispered loudly to Blake and Chloe.

"No one did!" Blake barked. "There's a lot about Mr. Todd Banks that we don't know."

Whatever beef there was between Blake and Khalil was beyond me, but as I watched Khalil shoot Blake another cold, hard and menacing stare, a chill ran down my spine.

Blake narrowed his eyes in return before pivoting and stomping out of the ballroom with an unopened bottle of Hennessy in one hand, two shot glasses in the other.

"I'm not a fan of your best man," Khalil spat as we approached the bar. "I can smell a snake a mile away and your boy is a dirty, two-legged snake. I thought I told you that before."

It was clear my best friend and my brother were on course for an inevitable collision, so I quickly shifted the conversation to safer grounds.

"So, what do you think of my fiancée? She looks pretty good, doesn't she?" I bragged.

As the bartender placed Khalil's beer on the coaster in front of him, he glanced toward Chloe as she beamed blissfully, conversing with a group of extended relatives.

"Beauty fades," he said with a nonchalant shrug. "It's always the gorgeous ones that you need to be careful of," he cautioned. "I mean, don't get me wrong, bruh," he continued, pausing to take a swig of his beer. "She is fine-looking, but she could be putting on a show for her audience. You did say she's a pastor, right?"

"Yeah, she's a pastor," I sounded back, deflated. I'd been hoping his perspective would squash my lingering doubts and convince me that getting married was the right thing to do. As I glanced around the immaculately decorated ballroom, everything looked perfect, but now that the moment had arrived, it seemed the past seven months had been too much of a whirlwind.

"Do you think I'm making a mistake by marrying her?" I asked him.

He looked me square in the eye. "Only you can answer that

question," he said directly. "If you don't want to marry her, then call it off."

"It's not that easy." I quickly backpedaled, a trace of panic lacing my voice.

"Why not?" he pushed. "Why would you marry someone you are not connected to?"

"Who said we didn't have a connection?" I shot back, though deep down, it was so obvious he was right. Chloe was a good woman, and I did love that about her, but if I was honest with myself, I was mostly attracted to her striking good looks and killer body.

"Hey, you asked." He shrugged again before chugging the rest of his beer.

"But look at all the people here celebrating with us," I protested defensively, not ready to let it go, sweeping my arm out to indicate the crowded ballroom. "Everyone here is counting on me. How can I possibly let so many people down?"

"Who cares about what these people think?" he retorted, placing his empty beer bottle on the bar. "This is your life. You have to live your life for yourself, bruh," he continued. "Don't live your life for no one else. At the end of it all, will anyone in this room matter?"

His comment hit home, causing the hairs on my arms to stand up.

He was right, but the idea of walking away from it all made me panicky. "But what will everyone think if I pull out now?" I asked. His comments were falling on deaf ears.

He turned to face me directly, placing both hands on my shoulders.

"You've got it backwards, bruh. The real question is, how will you live with yourself if you betray *yourself* by staying when you know it isn't right? Isn't that much more important than trying to please these phony-ass people?" He raised his eyebrows, challenging me.

"I'm not trying to please anyone!" I stepped back, taking offense. "Especially the people in this room."

Khalil was adamant. "Nice try, bruh, but being concerned with what others think of your choices is not living for yourself. When are you going to start living your own life and stop trying to please everyone else? When was the last time you made a decision for you, bruh?"

"I have made plenty of decisions for me," I tried to counter, stumbling over my words in my haste to spit them out.

"Okay," he said, still staring me down. "Let's hear one, then."

Trying to think on my feet, I quickly took stock of the recent decisions I'd made, the choices that had brought me to this day. As Khalil had pointed out moments earlier, my relationship with Chloe was built primarily on physical attraction, not the deep connection that should have been the foundation of a marriage. I thought of London again.

Yes, Chloe was beautiful—she even looked a little like London—but there was no question my instant connection with London had been stronger, more powerful, than anything with Chloe.

Is that the real reason I agreed to all this? I asked myself. Because I was trying to replace London with Chloe? I didn't have to answer. I'd only said yes to this marriage to escape the pressure from Blake and Chloe, not because I really wanted to tie the knot.

Pretending otherwise was a lie, though it hurt to admit it. Glancing at Khalil still awaiting my answer, I dug deeper. There was the fact that I was a successful attorney—surely that counted for something. But... had that been my dream? My decision? Though I hadn't thought about it in years, I suddenly remembered I'd wanted to become a history professor, not a lawyer.

I had only shifted gears at my mother's request. She had wanted a son who was an attorney and she'd been through so much, I couldn't disappoint her.

Preparing myself to be a lawyer hadn't been fun. The only thing that had helped me through was my fraternity, though I'd resisted joining at first. In fact, I realized wryly, the only reason I pledged was because Blake had done so, and he'd been begging me to join too.

Apparently, that hadn't really been my decision either.

Damn, I thought. I was running out of options, not liking the pattern that was obviously emerging. I shook it off, perhaps just needing to look back a little further. As I searched the recesses of my mind for something—anything—that I could tell Khalil was truly my own choice, there came a heap of painful memories of my father beating my mother.

I'd felt so helpless, so small and weak, so powerless. Countless times I'd called out to God, begged Jesus to protect my mother and make it stop. As the abuse had continued, I'd started to doubt God even cared. Eventually, I'd stopped praying altogether.

Apparently, having given up on God, my path became instead to please others, prioritizing their demands and preferences over mine. It seemed like a pretty monumental choice.

Was that the only choice I could claim as my own?

I stared at Khalil without speaking, completely at a loss for words, frozen in place, overwhelmed by this sudden realization. "You're a liar, bruh. You've been living for others while lying to and fooling yourself," he echoed my thoughts, calling me out with a brotherly smile. Despite his accusation, he wanted the best for me. "This may be a rehearsal dinner, but your *life* isn't a dress rehearsal. Time to take off your mask and start living your own life.

"You only get one." Khalil took a final swig from his second beer as I stood there, still speechless. "Don't mean to rain on your parade, bruh, but I gotta roll."

He punched me lightly on the arm, then turned on his heel. Moments later, he was gone.

Chapter 33

WITH A HALF-EMPTY bottle of Hennessy in his hand, Blake strolled over to the table where Chloe and I were now sitting. I had managed to pull myself together with the help of a few generous cocktails. Though my conversation with Khalil still lingered at the back of my mind, I was riding a pleasant buzz.

"TB," he announced grandly. "We need to talk."

"Talk about what?" He grabbed my empty cocktail glass and filled it brim full with Hennessy.

He raised his own brimming glass as he arrogantly scanned the room. "Here's to us," he shouted as the amber liquid sloshed dangerously. "And to everyone who wants to be like us!" Several others raised their glasses in return, joining in.

"Are you trying to get me drunk?" I asked in a low voice as he gulped his drink.

"Do you mind if I steal your fiancé for a moment?" Blake queried, directing his question at Chloe. "I promise to bring him back in one piece." He smiled broadly.

"Of course," she conceded as she flashed a grin in return. "Just have him back in time for the toast."

"Yes, boss!" he laughed.

"Todd, baby," Chloe beckoned. "Before you go, can I have a word with you?"

"What's up?" I said, tipping back my glass.

"Blake is drunk," she said quietly, but bluntly. "Please try to keep him from embarrassing us tonight, okay, honey?"

"Do you know how beautiful you look tonight?" I complimented. She was stressed, and it was up to me to help take the edge off.

"Why don't you tell me, handsome?"

"You are the most beautiful flower in the garden." I kissed her forehead.

"I am so in love with you, Mr. Banks," she said before kissing me hard.

"I'll be back in just a moment." I smiled before turning to Blake who was bouncing impatiently on his toes.

As we headed out of the ballroom, Blake grabbed me by the back of the arm. "I have a gift for you, TB," he exclaimed as he reached inside his blazer. He pulled out a marijuana joint the size of an index finger.

"My man!" I said excitedly.

"I couldn't let my boy go out without a last hurrah," he explained as he ushered me into a secluded alcove near the ballroom. He passed me the joint and lighter. "Fire up!"

I did as I was told. After just two hits, I was on cloud nine. "Where did you get this weed?" I asked, passing him the joint. "This is some high-powered stuff," I remarked, my eyes glued on the door to the ballroom. I'd never shared with Chloe that I smoked weed from time to time.

If she discovered I was getting high at our rehearsal dinner, all hell would break loose.

He ignored my question, taking a long puff before passing the joint back to me. "You're making a grave mistake by marrying Chloe," he stated.

"Why do you say that?" I asked, only halfway registering his comment. I was definitely feeling it. I glanced down at my wristwatch worriedly.

"Listen, TB," he said sternly. "Chloe isn't the woman for you. I think you need to put a halt to this wedding crap."

"Wait a minute." I held up my hand, pulling on the joint again. "Wasn't it your idea that we get married in the first place?"

"Yeah, true," he laughed. "But are you sure you know what you're committing to? It's the rest of your life we're talking about here. Are you sure you can trust her?"

"She's a pastor," I laughed back. "Of course, I can trust her. Besides, I thought you were happy for me. Don't tell me you're saying all this because you really did want to marry Chloe after all!"

"Nah. Chloe and I are just friends, nothing more. I just want to make sure that you've..."

He was cut short as the door to the ballroom swung open. Anticipating Chloe, my heart jumped into my throat, but only Monica strolled out.

"Put out the joint before she sees us," I clamored.

"No way," Blake refused, instead taking another hit. He blew the smoke toward Monica who was quickly heading our way.

"Hey, boys." She smiled.

"What's up ho—I mean Monica," Blake laughed. "You want to hit this?"

Rather than replying, she grabbed the joint with her perfectly manicured fingers and took a long pull. Blake turned to me and smiled.

"Wow," she said, exhaling over our heads. "This is the best weed I have ever smoked." She passed the joint back to me.

As I brought it to my lips, she added, "Chloe is looking for you and I don't think she would approve of you getting high on her special day."

She turned and headed back into the ballroom, shaking her ass with every step.

"Even though I don't like that ho," Blake sneered, "she does have a killer body. I would hit that all night."

"Do you think she will tell Chloe that I'm smoking?" I asked worriedly.

"No, but I'm sure the smell on your clothes will give it away, Mr. Attorney."

At that moment, my phone buzzed. "That's her, isn't it?"

"Hello?" I answered.

"Where are you, Todd?" Chloe asked. "Monica just told me that you and Blake are smoking pot and flirting with the hotel staff. Please tell me you are not going to make me the laughing stock of the church."

"I'll be right there," I told her.

Figuring I was already high out of my mind, I took one last hit off Blake's mega-joint before heading back into the ballroom. Chloe sat chit-chatting with her parents, all smiles until she laid eyes on me. Seconds later, she was headed my way.

"We need to talk," she hissed under her breath while pasting on a superficial smile.

I chugged the rest of my beer, cleared my throat and replied, "We don't have anything to talk about." It seemed the talk with Khalil, the numerous drinks I'd consumed and the high-grade weed now coursing through my bloodstream had taken effect; I'd managed to grow a pair.

"If you want to talk to someone, start with your friend, the snitch, about the weed she just smoked with us."

"So Monica was right. You have been smoking. Even your eyes are glazed over."

Grabbing me by the elbow, she led me out of the ballroom. As the door closed behind her, she spun to face me with a deeply troubled look.

"I'm sorry," I said automatically as her eyes began to water. Instead of comforting her, I reached inside my pants pocket for my Altoids and popped a few. "Please forgive me," I added. My voice sounded robotic.

She placed her hands on the sides of my face as she looked me in the eye. "Please promise me that you will never smoke again. I'm the pastor of the church and as my soon-to-be husband, you must set an example for those you will one day lead."

What did she mean, 'one day lead?' I thought slowly, waiting for my addled brain to catch up to the conversation. Suddenly, Blake and Monica appeared beside us.

"Is everything okay?" they rang in unison.

"Yeah, we're good," I said, mean-mugging Blake who had his hand over his mouth to muffle his laughter.

"What's so funny?" I mouthed at him.

He just shook his head and stepped closer to Chloe's side. "Are you sure you're okay, baby girl?" he asked as he wrapped his arm around her shoulder. He led her back into the ballroom as Monica trailed behind them, leaving me alone in the hallway.

What the hell just happened? I wondered. This night sure wasn't going as planned. Hoping it would all work itself out, I headed outdoors for a Black & Mild.

*****

Fifteen minutes later, I reluctantly re-entered the ballroom, still feeling as if heading straight for a failed marriage. Chloe and Monica were seated at the head table with Chloe's parents. Still unfit for conversation, I headed straight for the bar.

"Can I get a Corona and two Hennessy shots?"

"Right away." The bartender nodded.

"I'll have the same as the husband-to-be," Blake said to the bartender, coming up behind me and playfully jabbing me in the arm.

"This sucks, man," I told him. I tipped back my first shot as soon as it hit the bar. "I'm going to fail miserably as a husband."

"Relax, man," he laughed, grabbing one of his shots and knocking it back. "This is supposed to be a happy moment for you and your beautiful bride-to-be."

I nearly choked on my beer. Was he crazy? My boy needed to get his story straight. "Weren't you the one who just tried talking me out of getting married? Now you're Cupid?" I accused.

"Listen, T.B.," he said, taking down his second shot. "No one put a gun to your head. You could easily have said no, but you said yes. You seem keen to do it so I can only support you."

"What?" I shouted, way too loud. With all the back-and-forth, I was finding it hard not to strangle my best man. He was confusing me more with every passing second.

"Like I told you before, Chloe is not my choice for you, but if you believe she is the one, I support you."

"Why the change of heart?"

"As I said, you're my boy; I've nothing but love for you. Your happiness is important to me."

Just then, a hand gently settled on my arm, and I turned to find Chloe and Monica right behind us. I hoped the noise in the ballroom had kept my conversation with Blake private.

"Baby," she said, her eyes apologetic. "I'm sorry about earlier. I just want everything to be perfect for us."

"I do too," I told her, uncertain. "But I'm really tired of everyone telling me what to do and how to do it. I just want to be me."

"Yeah, yeah, yeah…" Blake chimed in. "You know you're a lucky man, TB." He smiled at Chloe. "Extremely lucky!"

"Yeah, mamacita," Monica echoed. "You two have got it good. Todd is the bomb.com!"

"I do love you, Chloe," I said, trying to keep my doubts out of my voice.

"And I love you too, baby."

She reached up and grabbed the back of my neck, kissing me hard.

"Papi." Monica jumped in with a clap of her hands. "You are the ting to her yang!" she exclaimed.

"Ting?" I reacted with a raised eyebrow. "Don't you mean yin to her yang?"

"No, silly," she chuckled. "It's ting, not yin."

At this, a nearby couple laughed.

"Yes, TB, you are her ting," Blake added.

It's yin, right? I thought. Second-guessing myself, I decided to let it go. I quickly swallowed my second shot of Hennessy and downed the rest of my beer.

Chapter 34

"SPEECH, SPEECH, SPEECH…" everyone rang out.

"Come on, baby." Chloe shook my arm. "Everyone's finished eating. It's time!"

"Time for what?"

"Time to tell everyone here how much we love them."

"Love?" I repeated dumbly. I didn't even *like* most of these people.

Grabbing me by the hand, she dragged me up to a small wooden podium located at the front of the ballroom. With nowhere to turn, I took a deep breath, put on a smile, and picked up the microphone.

Before I could utter a single word, Chloe coquettishly slipped the microphone from my hand. "Follow my lead." She winked, reminding everyone in the room who was wearing the pants.

A slight wave of humiliation engulfed me, but I brushed it off and stepped to the side as the natural charisma she displayed from the pulpit every Sunday took over.

As she thanked everyone for their support and their roles in bringing us to this point, I stood there in a daze, barely hearing her words. Instead, I stared at the elaborate crystal chandeliers dangling from the ballroom ceiling. Noticing Blake in the back, flirting with one of Chloe's cousins, I thought back to my single days. Life had seemed simple then.

That is, until I met London, and everything started changing. I pictured London's lovely face again as I had so many times before. It had been fifteen months since our first and only encounter, but it seemed as if we'd met just yesterday. Here I was celebrating my impending marriage to another woman while wondering if I'd ever see London again.

"Todd, Todd!" Chloe whispered as she nudged me. "Are you okay?"

Shaking myself out of my reverie, I nodded quickly. "Yeah, I'm good."

I shot her a half smile.

"Would you like to say a few words to our guests?" She laid the microphone on the podium and grabbed a seat next to Monica, leaving me standing there alone.

Gingerly, I picked up the mic. "Good evening, everyone," I said nervously, feeling the intoxicating effects of alcohol pulsing through my brain. Hoping I wouldn't make a fool of myself, I tried to gather my thoughts. "Hope you're all having a great time," I started out lamely.

"We would be if you weren't about to commit the greatest crime in the history of mankind." Laughter echoed through the room. Even the wait staff seemed amused. "It's never too late to run for the hills, TB!" Blake added.

"I love you too, Blake." I rolled my eyes and continued. "Chloe and I are honored that each of you has chosen to join us for our celebratory moment. Having all of you here is a genuine expression of how truly blessed we are," I continued, gaining confidence.

"Yeah, yeah, yeah! Enough of the mushy stuff, playboy," Blake heckled. "Kill the small talk and let us get back to the bar."

Chloe marched back up to the podium with a smile pasted on her face that came nowhere, close to reaching her eyes. "Will you tell your boy to keep his comments to himself?" she said through her teeth. "He is not Kevin Hart."

"Relax," I said under my breath. "And remember 'my boy' is your childhood friend. He's just having fun."

"Well, I don't think he is funny," she said loudly enough that her words were audible over the speaker system. "Give me the mic." She extended her hand.

"The boss lady has spoken!" Blake exclaimed, still laughing.

"We love you all so much," Chloe rang aloud, really selling it as she managed to shed a few counterfeit tears. "Even you, funny man." She pointed at Blake. "We are so grateful that God has blessed us by putting you in our lives. And to our parents, Todd and I promise to always put God first in our marriage."

"Amen!" everyone shouted in unison.

What does that mean, exactly? I wondered, trying to force my buzzed brain to compute. I brushed it off, figuring I'd sort it out later. As Chloe set down the microphone, I gave the bartender and DJ a thumbs up to get back to business. "Let's get this celebration started!"

With the bar open and the DJ inviting the crowd to the dance floor, the room looked more like a real wedding reception than a rehearsal dinner. More pensive than party-minded, I posted myself at the bar, sipping on another Corona, watching Chloe and Monica dance circles around another of my frat brothers, Josh Green.

A smooth-talking, blue-eyed guy with Michael Ealy good looks, Josh was a non-committal player type who owned a number of successful sports bars in the Atlanta area.

I'd had second thoughts about including him in the festivities but having learned how many of her friends and family Chloe was inviting, my numbers had needed a boost.

Thus, I'd added him as a groomsman. *At least he knows how to throw down and celebrate,* I reminded myself, signaling the bartender for another drink.

Chapter 35

"ARE YOU OKAY, TB?" Blake eyed me with a knowing look.

He'd always had the uncanny ability to read me. As I swigged my beer, I had a feeling I was about to receive a patented Blake Harden lecture.

"Of course, I'm okay," I lied. *How many lies does that make tonight?* a voice rang in my head. I ignored it, swigging my beer again. "I'm marrying the woman of my dreams, and my family and friends are here, celebrating this joyous occasion with me. What more could I ask?"

My words sounded forced even to me.

"I didn't know you and Josh were still friends," Blake commented as he watched Josh, Chloe and Monica shake it on the dance floor. He winked at me before lifting yet another shot glass to his lips. "Especially after he slept with your girl back in freshman year. What was her name again?" he asked, setting the shot glass on the bar. "Never mind." He waved before I could answer. "Doesn't matter. I just figured you'd never forgive him."

I sighed. He was right; Josh and I hadn't been close since that long-ago incident. But did Blake have to resurrect the past and open an old wound tonight? Why couldn't he just let it go?

"Listen," I said, ready to give him a taste of his own medicine. My gaze returned to the dance floor where the trio was still dancing. "If anyone should know about forgiveness, it should be you. Isn't that what your Bible says?" I tossed out, giving him a long sideways glance.

"Ha," he returned as he leaned over the bar and grabbed a bottle of Scotch while the bartender served up a martini down at the other end. "If you are not careful, TB, that blue-eyed devil will convince Chloe to stray, just like Eve," he told me, snickering at his own biblical reference.

"Yeah, right!" I tried to laugh it off. "It's been over fourteen years, man. None of us is the same as we were that long ago. We were kids back then."

He gave me another knowing look. "You are too smart to be stupid, TB." He shook his head. "Don't you know a leopard never changes its spots?"

Suddenly, Blake's head swiveled toward the dance floor. "That's the jam!" he shouted as the DJ started spinning the old-school hit, 'Jump,' by Kris Kross. He rushed onto the dance floor to join Chloe, Monica and Josh and the four of them pogoed to the beat.

Watching Chloe and the others jump around put a smile on my face; the old song took me back to an easier time.

Even the bartender joined in on the fun, bouncing as he mixed up a custom cocktail.

As the song ended, Monica meandered toward the bar while Chloe, Josh and Blake rolled into the next tune, still dancing.

"I don't like your friend Josh," Monica stated, grabbing my beer from the bar and chugging away. "He was trying to feel my booty."

"Well, you do have a big…" I stopped mid-sentence, shifting gears before I put my foot in my mouth. "I mean, you are very attractive."

"He is cute though," she hinted, ignoring my comment. "Kind of reminds me of a poor man's version of Michael Ealy," she added. "I'm sure he's not the perfect guy either."

As she continued to ramble on about Josh, I tuned her out and returned my gaze to the party. After a few more moments, Chloe and Blake were making their way toward the exit together.

"Hold on, girl," Monica screeched in my ear, causing me to cringe.

She set down my now-empty beer bottle and dashed toward the two of them. "Talk to you later, Papi," she called to me over her shoulder.

"Can I get another Corona?" I instructed the bartender. As I waited, my thoughts wandered back to my earlier conversation with Khalil. Over the last several months, I'd come to respect his opinion. Given the way this evening was going, I was starting to think he was right.

Maybe I did need to figure out what I really wanted for myself. Maybe, just maybe, the person I'd spent most of my life deceiving was myself.

The bartender returned, interrupting my musing as he placed my drink on a coaster. Before I could pick up my beer, Josh approached and took the seat next to me.

"Thanks for inviting me out tonight, Banks," he said, his blue eyes locked on mine. "You are a very lucky man. Your fiancée is gorgeous," he added with a gleam in his eye.

"Thanks," I responded, my voice flat. My thoughts were tangled in Khalil's accusation that I was a liar, building my life just to please others.

"So why now?" he asked as he grabbed my Corona off the coaster and took a sip. I sighed. I was getting tired of people stealing my drinks without asking.

"What do you mean, why now?" I replied, signaling the bartender for yet another beer.

"Well," he began, "from what I hear, you've got it pretty good. You've got a job you like and a killer salary. I understand that your digs are top-notch, and your woman is one of the hottest I've ever met. You are living the dream, man," he explained, tipping back the bottle and chugging it down. "Not that I mind free drinks on your tab." He grinned at me. "But why would you settle down? Why now? You could still have all this and be single."

I looked at him, surprised at the question. Marrying Chloe had seemed like the thing to do, so I'd rolled with it. My answer was my best shot.

"Well, I'm thirty-three years old. I've never been married and believe it's the right time," I parroted. My rote reply sounded dull even to me, but I had no better answer to give.

"Is that all you got?" he questioned. "What about love? Why her? What is it about your fiancée that told you she was the one?" His questions were coming rapid-fire.

"Well, I do love her," I retorted, though hearing the lack of conviction behind my words. "I just know she's the one?" My statement sounded more like a question.

"But how?" he pressed. "How do you know she, and not someone else, is 'the one?'"

"I just do," I said slowly, dumbfounded that I'd never asked myself this question.

"So, you just knew you were supposed to get married because, what, God told you so?" He snickered, grabbing my second beer as the bartender set it down. His words hit home harder than he intended; this time, the stolen drink passed me by. Under my collar, the temperature was hot.

Pulling at my collar didn't help, so I took the easy way out.

"I'll be right back," I said hurriedly. "The restroom's calling." I slid off my barstool and dashed toward the exit.

Chapter 36

I PUSHED THROUGH the ballroom's heavy doors, quickly finding the restroom, slipping inside. I headed into one of the stalls, turned the lock and leaned my forehead against the cool metal door as Josh's question ricocheted around in my skull. Having convinced myself I was doing the right thing in asking Chloe to marry me, all the pieces had been slotting into place, but had God actually told me Chloe was the one? In my panic, the answer was unclear.

I may not have been a church regular, but God would not let me get this far if it wasn't right.

Alone for the first time all night, it was time to get some answers from God direct. Preparing myself for some serious impromptu communion, voices were coming ever nearer.

The bathroom door burst open and in walked a group of chattering women. The blood drained from my face; I'd somehow stumbled into the women's room in my haste to escape Josh.

I froze, afraid to make a sound that would give me away.

Would they see my feet under the stall? I gingerly tiptoed backwards until my calves bumped against the toilet. As I stood there, barely breathing, their conversation turned to Josh.

It seemed there was no escape.

"Girl, I would let that blue-eyed man do whatever he wanted to me," laughed a woman's voice I didn't recognize.

"Yeah, so would I," rang another voice I thought was Monica. "He is so fine."

"He may look like an angel, but the two of you are a mess," another voice spoke. "You all need Jesus!"

Their laughter echoed through the room as a bead of sweat ran down my temple. "Let's go find him!" Monica suggested. Seconds later, they were gone.

When the coast was clear, I slowly opened the stall door and cautiously approached the exit. Laying my ear against the bathroom door, I waited until there were no longer voices on the other side. Pushing the door open an inch, then another, confirmed there was no one nearby.

Relief overwhelmed me at stepping out into freedom again.

That was a close one.

Just as the door closed behind me, several ladies from Porsche's Salon approached.

"Congratulations, Todd," Riley exclaimed, shooting me a perfect smile. "I'm really happy for you and Chloe. The two of you look so cute together."

"Thanks." I smiled. "I really appreciate you saying that."

"Yeah, you do look great together. But are you sure you know what you're getting yourself into, Mr. Attorney?" Angie asked as she tilted her head to the side, staring up at me. "Pastors can be a lot of work. You sure you can handle it? Have you prayed about it? Did God tell you Chloe is the one?"

Can she read minds? Her questions were hitting too close to home. I tried to plaster on a poker face as she kept tossing questions out, one after another.

"Leave him alone, Ang." Riley laughed. "He's marrying a pastor. They met at the church. Of course, he's prayed for the Lord to help him do the right thing."

As we began the short walk back to the ballroom, Sydney chimed in. "Congrats." She smiled, looking me up and down. "I wish you and Chloe nothing but the best. She deserves a good man like you."

"Thanks," I said, surprised at her compliment. "I appreciate it."

But her words rang in my head. *A man 'like' me. She didn't say 'she deserves you.' There are many men 'like me', so it doesn't have to be me then, does it?*

I held the door open, inviting them all to rejoin the rehearsal party.

Riley and Sydney darted toward the dance floor to join in on the 'Electric Slide,' but Angie hung back. She pulled me to the side.

"Listen, Todd," she said frankly, turning to look me in the eyes. "I know I don't know you very well, but if there's one thing you should know 'bout me, it's that I do have a powerful relationship with Jesus Christ, my Lord and Savior."

"That's cool," I replied generically, waiting to see where she was going with it.

"But if you are not ready to get married, then don't."

"What do you mean?" She had my full attention.

"The eyes are the window to the soul, my brother," she stated. "The eyes are the window to the soul. That's all I'm sayin'. And your eyes tell me that Chloe isn't the one."

"But I love her," I said fruitlessly. "She has to be the one since Lon…"

"Since what?" She searched my eyes.

"Since London is where I booked our honeymoon," I covered, lying through my teeth.

"If you say so. Just trust that still, small voice within," she said. "And remember, this is your life. *Everyone* here," she gestured toward the teeming dance floor, "wants the best for you and Chloe, including me. But what that means is between you and God."

With that, she was gone.

Chapter 37

AT 10:30 A.M. the next morning, I was torn out of a deep sleep by the incessant beeping of my old-school alarm clock on the bedside table. Damn. I glanced at those red numbers, rubbing my eyes. That thing had been going off for two hours.

Oversleeping on my wedding day? Really?

Moreover, I couldn't believe I was actually about to be married.

I'd managed to drown my doubts with ample quantities of Hennessy last night, but this morning, they were back in full force. Josh's and Angie's questions still echoed in my mind.

Glancing down, I noticed my rehearsal dinner outfit, now abysmally wrinkled after passing out in it the night before. *No more drinking for me,* I thought as I pulled myself out of bed, holding my pounding head and gingerly making my way to the bathroom.

With less than an hour before I had to be at the church to meet up with Blake, Khalil, and Josh, I barely had time to get ready. I quickly got undressed and into the shower.

There'd be time to straighten my mind out on the drive over.

At 10:58 a.m., I was dressed and ready to go—in record time given my morning routine usually took over an hour. Grabbing my tuxedo and patent leather shoes from the closet, I lifted my car keys from the table by the door, reluctantly heading out to my car to face the inevitable.

As I pulled out, the weight of the choice I was about to make felt crushingly heavy, in need of a lifeline. So I'd call the one person I thought might be able to help me.

The phone rang three times. "Hello?"

"Hey, Mom." My voice trembled. "It's me, Todd."

"I know who this is," she retorted, immediately picking up on my uneasiness. "I gave birth to you, remember?" She expected me to laugh.

Nothing like that happened. Only silence. I envisioned her standing in her kitchen with her hand on her hip. "Aren't you supposed to be at the church getting ready for your big day?"

"Yeah, I'm on my way there now," I responded hurriedly, attempting to come up with a clever way to tell her of my need to call the wedding off. As my heart pounded against my ribcage, I swallowed hard, trying to find words to succinctly explain it all.

But there was nothing but the truth.

Finally, the words came tumbling free. "I can't marry her, Mom. She's not the one."

Though my heart felt a tiny bit lighter as the words left my lips, the silence that followed lingered in the air like smoke in a windowless room. For several heart-stopping moments, she didn't utter a single word though her breathing came heavy down the line.

Several times, my mouth opened to speak, only to concede there was nothing else to say.

The silence grew longer still. What exactly was going through her mind?

Whatever... I'd learned early in childhood that the longer Mom remained quiet, the more deeply she consulted with God. Interrupting was unacceptable, so I held my tongue.

When I finally heard her say, "Amen," the rubber was about to meet the road. "Have you lost your damn mind, boy? Don't you dare leave that woman standing at that altar."

So much for support, I thought, accelerating as the light before me turned green. I knew better than to fight Mom when she was this adamant, but I couldn't back down from my own self either, not with my whole life on the line.

I tried to explain further. "Mom, this has all happened too fast. I still barely know Chloe and signing up for the rest of my life with a woman I'm unsure about just seems all wrong. It sounds dramatic, but it feels like I'm committing suicide and know I'm not ready to die.

"What should I do, Mom?" I pleaded.

"You know what to do. Don't make the wrong choice. Do not leave that woman standing at the altar," she stated firmly a second time. "And if it doesn't work out, you can always get a divorce," she continued, her voice lower.

"A divorce?" I was floored. "How can you even say that? You were the one who taught us that divorce was not an option in God's eyes. I know how many beatings you took just trying to keep our family together!"

"Listen, Son." Her voice grew soft and loving. "You're right; I stayed too long, but that's in the past. You know I don't want to see you divorced. But if I were in your shoes, I would marry her. She seems like an incredible woman and the fact that she is the pastor of a church tells me the two of you will be equally yoked as followers of Christ."

My gut tightened at her calm assumption that I'd accepted Jesus as my Lord and Savior, especially since I'd managed to avoid revisiting church since before Chloe and I got engaged.

Chloe's world was not my own; that much was evident.

My brain had generated a series of excuses I couldn't even recall right now. "Now take your ass to that church and marry that beautiful woman of God," she finished with vehemence.

As I hung up, my one lifeline had done me no good.

With Mom against me, my thoughts were even more conflicted than before this call. I still couldn't see a way to go through with it given my feelings, but I also couldn't see a way out, other than just manning up and telling Chloe the truth.

My heart rate accelerated at the thought.

The one with Chloe was a conversation I absolutely did not want to have.

Out of options and out of time, I needed to floor it straight to the church to make it in time to meet Blake, Josh, and Khalil. Instead, I found myself turning into the parking lot of Render's Coffee Shop on Columbus Avenue.

In a parking spot, I sat for a moment with the engine running. Suddenly, I realized I did have one more option left, though it was a ridiculously long shot.

Still, it had seemed to work for me before, so it was worth a try. Closing my eyes, I bowed my head and prayed. "God, if Chloe is not the woman that you desire to be my wife, please make it clear to me within the next thirty minutes." I opened my eyes and glanced around, hoping the answer would be immediately obvious. Everything at the coffee shop seemed like business as usual. I sighed, rolling my eyes at my pathetic prayer. But I slipped off my TAG Heuer wristwatch and started counting down the minutes just in case.

Fifteen minutes later, God was still keeping me waiting in silence. My frustration was rising as seconds ticked by. Clearly, God needed a reminder of how serious this was.

"You now have just *fifteen* minutes to show me a sign. Is Chloe the one or not?"

There was a profound irritation in my voice. Needing to chill out, so I turned off the car ignition, reclined my seat and lit up a cigar, waiting on an almighty response.

An older model Chevy Cavalier pulled into the empty spot next to mine, and an elderly woman with long white hair looked over at me and smiled.

I shot her a half smile in return, then peered back down at my watch. With twenty seconds remaining before the thirty minutes were up, I sighed again and started the car.

It seemed my prayer would go unanswered. No surprise.

And I threw the car in reverse.

There was some peculiar noise! Just when I didn't need a vehicle breakdown… the strange knocking was loud. I glanced out my rearview mirror and jumped in my seat.

That elderly woman was now standing next to my car, smiling at me again.

I immediately pulled back into the parking space, rolled down the window and stared up at her. "Can I help you?"

"Hello, son," she said in a motherly tone. Her blue eyes were bright as they held my gaze. "I have a message for you." She opened her purse and handed me a folded-up piece of paper. Without another word, she hopped back inside her car and quickly pulled out of the parking lot.

I watched her Chevy grow smaller out of my rearview until she was gone.

That was odd. I unfolded the scrap of paper, its words jumping off the surface: **CHOOSE LIFE OR DEATH**. My hands started to shake as the blood drained from my face.

I quickly dropped the scrap with its condemning words into an empty cupholder and grasped the steering wheel with both hands, sucking in several slow, deep breaths.

Despite my efforts, my heart rate continued to fly.

I was in no condition to drive, so turned off the car's engine again and opened the door. At the last second, I grabbed the little note from the cupholder, unwilling to let it out of my sight until I figured out what it meant. It was a message, no one could deny that. But what did it mean?

I stumbled inside Render's Coffee Shop as if I had seen a ghost, making my way in a daze to the end of a long line of customers waiting to order.

For once, I was grateful for the wait; my mind was spinning. My fingers groveled again in my pocket, unfurling the paper scrap, staring… raking my mind for answers.

I was pulled out of my reverie by someone tapping my shoulder. "Excuse me," rang the voice of a woman. "Are you going to place your order or just stand there all day?"

How rude!

"Huh?" The seemingly interminable line had disappeared in front of me.

Slipping the piece of paper into my pants pocket, I turned to apologize to those behind.

Before I could open my mouth, my gaze connected with the woman who had been tapping me on the shoulder. Surprise covered her features as my jaw dropped. A cold rush traveled down my spine, top to bottom, and my lungs held onto their breath. I almost dropped to the floor.

"London?"

Chapter 38

"TODD?" SHE EXCLAIMED as her eyes danced with mine.

"What are you doing here?" I shouted, not caring that a number of heads in the coffee shop turned curiously toward us at my outburst. "Where have you been?" I blurted desperately. I searched her face for answers. They were stupid, inane questions.

"What am I doing here? Looking for you. Where have I been? Looking for you."

It was like hearing a heavenly angel speak, and the words held me enraptured. She spoke as she reached for my hand, never taking her eyes off mine.

"What have you been up to? How have you been? Where have you been?" I couldn't seem to get my words out fast enough, like a kid with his first crush, flummoxed,

"I have been well." She flashed a breathtaking smile.

"You look amazing," I complimented.

She was dressed in a gray knee-length pencil skirt, a matching vest over a white button-up shirt and black high heel pumps, displaying her athletic legs beautifully.

She smiled again. "And you look like you stepped right out of Sports Illustrated."

"You like?" I said, puffing up my chest a bit under her seeming interest in my navy and white Nike sweatsuit and matching sneakers.

"Very much," she flirted.

With a million questions flying through my mind, I was trying to choose a direction for the conversation when it dawned on me that I still didn't know London's last name. "Can you please tell me what your last name is?" I beseeched.

"It's Mahone," she said and chuckled. "London Gabrielle Mahone."

Finally, I thought. "Beautiful. And my last name is Banks. Todd 'no middle name' Banks." We laughed in unison.

As our grins subsided and a comfortable silence fell between us, my heartbeat was finally returning to normal. The easy smile on her face mirrored my own.

"It was meant to be," she murmured softly. "Thank you, Jesus."

"I thought I had lost you forever," I said in a low voice. I wasn't sure I'd spoken loud enough for her to hear, but she gripped my hand a little tighter.

"If the stars are aligned, I won't be hard to find," she said. "Remember those words, Todd?"

"I'll never forget them. But did it have to take an eternity for those damn stars to line up?" I mockingly complained.

"I was starting to feel the same way," she laughed, leading me by the hand to a nearby table. Out of the corner of my eye, I noticed a number of heads pivoting to follow us across the room; our unexpected rendezvous had captured the attention of our fellow patrons.

Who cared if they eavesdropped? It was a pretty remarkable situation.

Seating myself across the small table from London, I removed my wallet from my jacket pocket and handed her one of my business cards, watching her face as she read it.

"You're an attorney?" she asked, looking up at me quickly. She seemed surprised.

I nodded. "I figured the outfit I was wearing the day we met gave it away," I joked.

"You are a very funny man, Todd 'no middle name' Banks," she grinned. "But unfortunately, I don't think of a blazer and a sweater when I envision a lawyer. I think of a crisply tailored suit. But there was something special about you when we first met," she said, slipping my card inside her purse and pulling out one of her own. I had a feeling she was talking about more than my wardrobe. "God has amazing plans for your life," she stated, handing me her card.

I glanced down to see I was holding a bright, but elegant card. "You're an artist?" I asked, purposefully ignoring her comment about God. He and I were due for a serious conversation, even if He had finally brought it upon himself to answer my last heartfelt message after all.

All the answers I wanted still hadn't fallen into place, but with the mysterious note from the elderly woman still in my pocket and London sitting in front of me, I no longer doubted whether God was involved in my life at all. He was here all right and listening to me.

"I prefer to call myself a painter," London clarified. She removed an iPad from her purse and flipped open the cover. "Here is some of my work if you care to scroll through."

"Impressive," I remarked as I scanned through paintings of former President Barack Obama, musician B.B. King and characters Okoye and Shuri from the blockbuster hit Black Panther. More impressive still were her self-portraits. I found myself taken aback by the intensity in each one; they were absolutely stunning. "Are any of these for sale?" I pressed, handing her the iPad.

"Yes," she replied, slipping the iPad back inside her purse. "But not for you."

"But I still owe you for the gift you gave me," I stated. Noticing the question on her face at my comment, I reached behind me into the backpack slung over the back of my chair and pulled out the scarf she had given me the day we met. Her eyes widened in surprise.

"You still have it?" she questioned, though the answer was obvious. "But why would you have it with you today?" Incomprehension rested in her features as she stared at me.

"Like my American Express card." My eyes danced with hers again. "I never leave home without it."

She reached out and ran her fingers over the soft material.

"I thought surely you would have tossed it."

"How could I chuck away such an important memento? It

was all I had to remind me that we actually met, that it wasn't just a dream that day on the train. Can I share something else?"

"Anything."

"Do you want to know what I remember most about that day?"

"What's that?"

"The sparkle in your eyes." I smiled. "You have the most beautiful eyes I have ever seen."

"I bet you say that to all the girls," she teased, leaning back.

"Nope." I shook my head, leaning forward to maintain our closeness. "Only you."

"Do you want to know why I think you believe I have the most beautiful eyes?" She leaned in again and this time, grabbed hold of my hands, squeezing gently.

"I do, very much."

"It's because when I look at you, I actually see you, Todd."

As I stared into her eyes, I knew exactly what she meant. I smiled and relaxed, allowing the easy silence to grow between us again. I looked down at her card, trying to imagine London at work, painting another masterpiece. Before my mind could wander too far, a flurry of movement over London's shoulder caught my eye. The elderly woman who had handed me the cryptic note less than an hour earlier was waving at me from across the room.

As she slowly approached our table, it suddenly dawned on me why she looked so familiar. I'd seen her before today—she had been on the train the same day I'd met London.

A second chill ran down my spine.

Finally arriving in front of us, the old woman patted London on the shoulder, then she smiled at me. "Don't let her get away this time," she cautioned in a low tone. "Fate has brought the two of you together again."

"I won't," I promised. "I learned my lesson last time," I said with a smirk.

"Fate will not come knocking again!" she exclaimed. Without further comment, she turned and wandered away from the table. I took the reminder and turned my attention to London who was looking at the old woman with an amused smile.

"London." I held her right hand in both of mine as if it were a prized possession. "Will you join me for a cup of coffee?" I asked, ready to make things different this time around.

"I will," she said with a smile, allowing me to escort her back up to the checkout counter.

Chapter 39

AFTER PICKING UP our drinks, London and I made our way out to the coffee shop's patio, hoping for a little privacy from the curious eyes and ears inside. A taxicab sat on the curb about fifty feet from Render's. It took me a moment to process the glaring advertisement plastered across its side, but it featured a woman in a voluminous wedding dress. I froze. What about Chloe and the vows I'd promised to take in just a few short hours? She hadn't even crossed my mind once since London had tapped my shoulder in the coffee shop.

Suddenly, the dream I'd felt I'd been in since looking up to see London's face shattered around me, reality crashing down in its place. My pulse sped up and my breathing grew shallow while panic kicked in. I looked over at London as she set her cup down on a nearby table. There was no way I could hide the fact that I was practically a married man.

Don't tell her! one voice insisted. *You'll make her run!* But another was quick to counter. *You must tell her the truth. No more lies!* For once, the second was the more compelling.

Recalling my conversation with Khalil, I knew I hadn't been honest with myself or others for much of my life, unable to count the number of lies that had brought me to this moment, but despite all of them, God had brought London back to me. It was time to come clean.

I slowly lowered myself to join London at the little metal table. Leaning in close, I took her hands. "London?" I began, feeling my heart knocking violently against my ribcage.

"Yes, Todd?" She gently rubbed her thumbs back and forth across the backs of my hands and stared deep into my eyes.

"I have something very important to tell you," I began, exhaling slowly.

"I'm listening."

I took a deep breath. No more lies, I reminded myself. "I'm getting married this afternoon at Park Street Church," I rushed out.

"Married?" She stood quickly, bumping the table and sloshing coffee over the edge of her cup. She stared down at me uncomprehendingly. "When… I mean, how… What the…"

"Her name is Chloe. She's a wonderful woman," I added, hoping a few more details would somehow help.

"Why didn't you tell me earlier?" London accused. She clutched her bag to her chest, then pivoted and started to make her way out of the enclosed patio.

"Wait." I followed. I couldn't bear to see her walk away again. "There's more."

"More?" She spun back to face me as her eyes welled. "What more can there possibly be? What? You're moving abroad? She's pregnant? What?"

A lone tear rolled down her cheek. "Why were you looking for me if you were committed to getting married?" she asked hopelessly. "All those times I searched for you on that train… I was a fool to think you were the one I had prayed for."

Another tear rolled gently down her face.

"I'm sorry, London," I said, slipping my hand back into hers. She allowed it, but barely seemed to notice. The despair on her face broke my heart; there had to be a means to take away the pain I'd caused. I opened my mouth, unsure of what I was about to say. "London, I love…" I began without thinking. Before I could complete the sentence, I froze.

"You what?" she queried, her eyes wide at my partial declaration. "What or who do you love? Your bride-to-be?" Her face twisted as she spit out the words, more tears belying her pain.

"Look, I have never met a woman like you," I said lamely, unable to finish my declaration, but not knowing what else to say. *Just tell her the truth,* asserted the small voice within.

Just tell her that you love her! Now!

I swallowed hard, trying to force down the lump in my throat. I opened my mouth, wanting to give her the words she needed and deserved, but nothing came out. The intensity of the moment was too much. "Please forgive me." I caved. My eyes began to water. "I'm so sorry."

She stood for a moment, then threw her arms around me briefly and squeezed tightly.

"It was nice seeing you again, Todd," she declared in a detached manner, her voice partially muffled against my tracksuit. She released me quickly. "Good luck with it all!"

And with that, she turned and walked away.

Chapter 40

I REMAINED FROZEN in place for several long minutes after London disappeared. Finally, I dragged myself to the church. Two short hours later, I found myself standing at the front of it with Blake, Josh, and Khalil flanking me as we stared down the still empty aisle.

Sporting matching black tuxedos, crisp white shirts, white bowties, and black patent leather tuxedo shoes, we looked ready for a magazine photo shoot.

Shielding my eyes from the glaringly bright spotlights, I peered into the crowded church wondering what the hell I was doing up here. My breathing was shallow and fast, my heart was racing, and I kept wiping my palms on the sides of my pants, trying to keep them reasonably dry.

The minutes dragged on.

The pastor, a dark-skinned, distinguished gentleman dressed in a formal black robe, turned to me. "Today is your big day." He smiled kindly. "Just follow my lead."

I nodded in agreement, wiping my palms again and stifling the urge to run the back of my hand across my forehead as well.

Blake leaned over to whisper loudly in my direction. "I can't believe you're going through with it," he said through his teeth. "You are crazier than I thought," he chuckled aloud.

"What do you mean?" I whispered over my shoulder at him.

"I cannot believe you're about to marry the same woman who accepted my proposal not even a year ago," he reminded, malice in his tone. "Desperate times really do equal desperate measures. Guess you gave up hope on your dream girl from the train. What's her name again?"

"London," I replied in a low voice, clenching my fists. It was seriously not the moment for this. Who the hell did he think he was, mocking me as I stood up here, about to make the biggest promise of my life? I tried to keep the emotion off my face, but I was sure every one of the more than 200 friends, family and loved ones filling the church could tell I was upset.

"I told you he was a snake," Khalil chimed in, inclining his head in Blake's direction. "Don't worry, bruh. I got you."

"I didn't know she dated Blake," Josh whispered loudly from the other side of Khalil. "But either way, she's a pastor, so I'm sure you two prayed about all this."

I lowered my gaze. Yes, I had prayed, albeit last minute. But look where that had gotten me. As I sighed to myself, London's face was clear in my mind, devastated at the news of my impending marriage. I couldn't forget the way life had drained from her face when I'd told her.

Reliving that conversation tore at my heart, but my mind kept dragging her pained expression right to the forefront of my thoughts.

I glanced back at my groomsmen and noticed Khalil scanning the crowd. Feeling my stare, he directed his attention to me, left his place in line, stepped over to me and dropped his hands on my shoulders. "Listen, bruh." He was all business. "If you don't want to get married today, you don't have to. To hell with all these phonies. This is your life and only you can choose. But if you betray your conscience by marrying a woman you don't love and don't want to marry, just know it will be no one's fault, but your own."

"I know," I replied, meeting his eyes and nodding. I glanced toward the pastor staring directly at me. I shrugged and mumbled, "Just got cold feet."

"Seriously, bruh. When are you going to stop giving your power to others?" Khalil pressed, still holding me by the arms. "I don't want to see you throw your life away. You've got to stand on your own two feet and make your own decisions."

The pastor, who obviously could hear our conversation, glared at Khalil. "Can you get back to your post?" he directed imperiously. "The bride will be appearing soon."

Khalil seemed unruffled. "Think about what I said," he reminded me, shooting the pastor a menacing glare before stepping back in line.

Khalil had shared similar words the night before, but now, standing at the front of the church, his reminders seemed even heavier.

London's heartbroken face popped again into my mind and my chest began to ache.

As a trickle of sweat tracked down my temple, I spotted my mother in the front pew, eyeing me. She leaned over and whispered to my sisters, Tena and Sade. Sade shook her head. "He doesn't want to marry her," Mom's lips read. "He is settling."

She shrugged.

"Are you okay?" Mom mouthed toward me, her face etched with concern.

"Yes." I nodded back, finally giving in and wiping the sweat from my brow with the back of my hand. What else could I say? My time was up, and it sure felt like the choice had already been made. Whether I meant to or not, following others had brought me here and now I had no way out. I couldn't save myself under the watchful eyes of everyone in the church.

This must be how Mom had felt when Dad beat her. As if she had no escape. But whenever Mom had been in trouble, she'd turned to Jesus and aside from the couple of little last-ditch prayers I'd managed over the past few months, I'd turned my back on Him years ago.

A lifetime of rejection surely meant it was too late for me.

Still, as I stared down the aisle awaiting my future, there was nothing left to lose—and maybe, just maybe, everything to gain. I took a deep breath and closed my eyes.

I was ready to pray the biggest prayer of my life, this time without any ultimatums.

"Dear Jesus," I began haltingly, my voice low. "I know I haven't been to church lately, but I've been told I will be saved if I confess with my mouth and believe in my heart you are Lord.

"Well, I sure feel like I need saving, so today, in front of all of these witnesses, whether they can hear me or not, I confess that I believe in you. I've made a mess of everything, and I don't know how to make things work out, but I trust your path for me."

Feeling there wasn't much else to say, I opened my eyes.

"Are you okay, son?" the pastor murmured worriedly in my direction.

I looked over at him wondering if I even knew the answer to his question. But as I opened my mouth to respond, a strange sense of calmness overcame me, one that hadn't been there before.

"Yes, I'm fine," I replied with a genuine smile. For the first time in my life, there was peace, as if my steps from this moment forward were sure to be divinely directed.

I smiled to myself as the organist began playing. The first few chords of music echoed through the church and Chloe's bridesmaids began to file in. As soon as the bridal party was fully in position, the organist shifted into 'Here Comes the Bride.'

Chloe appeared, her caramel skin glowing in perfect contrast against the bright white satin of her fitted gown. As she stepped forward, escorted by her father, her radiance hit me so powerfully I had to remind myself to breathe.

Slowly and gracefully, she took her first steps down the aisle.

Surely, there could be no one more beautiful, I told myself. The quick twist deep in my gut was probably just normal pre-marital nerves. Chloe was gorgeous and as everyone had told me, I was lucky to be marrying her. I took a deep breath and let it out slowly, trying to bring back the calmness of moments earlier.

"You lucky bastard," Blake whispered from behind me. I didn't get his irritation since he and Chloe had both told me there was nothing between them, but I let it go.

Blake's actions and attitude had grown more and more unpredictable; nothing he said came as a surprise anymore. It seemed Khalil might even be right in his assessment.

Another pair of eyes was staring me down; it was Khalil, watching me closely. "Don't be fooled by her good looks," he murmured. "This is your life you're choosing." I frowned briefly.

I'd made my choice, hadn't I? Chloe was obviously perfect, and I was the envy of every man in the church.

As Chloe drew nearer, the calmness I had felt slipped further away, replaced by a sudden anxiety. The pressure inside built up uncomfortably, an unexpected tear escaping my right eye.

"He's crying," rang the voice of an older woman seated in the front pew.

Crying? I thought, quickly wiping the tear away. It wasn't clear which of my jumbled emotions was to blame, but it didn't feel like a tear of joy. The peace I'd felt earlier was now completely gone; my heart was flying, my breathing so rapid I was starting to feel lightheaded.

I wiped my palms on the sides of my pants once more, hoping Chloe's beauty was captivating enough that no one would notice me wrestling with these unpredictable emotions.

Finally, Chloe and her father drew to a halt in front of us. As the organist played the final notes of the bridal chorus, the pastor extended his arms with palms facing upward.

Looking at Chloe, he smiled and said, "We are gathered here today before God to witness the joining of Chloe Patterson and Todd Banks. Who gives this woman to be married to this man?"

"I do," barked Mr. Patterson. Removing her hand from his arm, he planted a soft kiss to Chloe's forehead. "I love you, baby girl."

"I love you too, Daddy."

Taking a few short steps, Mr. Patterson reached me and extended his hand. His piercing look told me I was about to receive more than a handshake. "You better take very good care of my baby," he whispered, squeezing my hand tightly. "If you don't," he continued, lowering his voice further, "my friends Smith & Wesson will be paying you a visit."

I wasn't sure if he was kidding or not, so I nodded curtly and offered him a tight smile before he stepped back to take his seat on the front pew. Chloe stepped closer to face me.

After a quick, but powerful opening prayer reminding everyone in the room that marriage was a serious commitment before God, the pastor opened his Bible and began his wedding sermon, citing scriptures that encouraged us to honor the sacred covenant we were about to accept.

"There's no turning back now, TB," Blake resounded. His voice was loud enough for the pastor and the whole bridal party to hear. "I cannot believe you are really going through with it."

"Whatever, man," I whispered back. Chloe was staring him down with daggers in her eyes, clearly offended at the disrespectful interruption. I took another deep breath to steady myself, trying to absorb at least some of the pastor's message.

Finally, he concluded the sermon. "I love you, Mr. Banks," Chloe whispered quickly, squeezing my hands.

"Okay, church," the pastor said as he closed his Bible. "Before we head into the vows, we have one final question to ask you as witnesses to this joining. This is always the part of the ceremony that worries me most." He smiled, provoking a smattering of chuckles from the pews, though I didn't see anything funny in his comment. "Before Todd and Chloe make their commitment before God, I must ask," he said as he peered into the crowd, "is there anyone in this church who believes these two souls should not be joined together? If so, please speak now, or forever hold your peace." I took a deep breath and held it, nerves tangling my stomach. This was it.

As silence fell over the crowd, heads swiveled as everyone waited to see if some brave soul would interrupt our union. Chloe squeezed my hands a little tighter and smiled as we waited.

But no one said a word.

The seconds dragged and sweat popped out on my forehead. I peered nervously over at Mom who was impatiently bouncing her leg up and down. She nodded at me encouragingly. "I'm so proud of you," her lips read. But rather than calming me, my pulse increased in response.

How could she be proud of me as the liar I was, standing here in front of everyone, about to say 'I do' to the wrong woman? I was ashamed I didn't have the courage to stop this charade once and for all. I grabbed the handkerchief from my pocket, thankful I'd thought to stuff it in there at the last minute.

Anxiously, I reached up and blotted the sweat from my face.

"Are you okay?" the pastor asked as I tucked the handkerchief back in my pants pocket.

"What's that?" Chloe asked at the same time, using her free hand to point at a crumpled piece of paper lying on the floor by my left foot.

Without pause, I knelt down, picked up the paper and opened it.

Chapter 41

'CHOOSE LIFE OR DEATH!' jumped out at me. Despite feeling hot and sweaty only moments earlier, a chill ran down my spine. How had the note from my meeting with London ended up in my tuxedo pocket? I wasn't sure, but the timing was too precise to ignore it.

God was trying to get my attention... again.

"It's nothing," I said quickly as I tucked the note in my pocket. Chloe scowled but said nothing. I tried to keep a poker face as my mind flew, attempting to put the pieces together.

What choice do I have? I thought desperately. We were about to say our vows.

This marriage was practically a done deal.

As I looked down at Chloe's hand in mine, contemplating what was about to come, my earlier rendezvous with London flashed through my mind yet again. I couldn't believe I had gotten her back after so many months, only to lose her again a moment later.

Remembering her broken face cut my heart deeply. *How will I ever find her now?* I wondered sadly, forgetting where I was for a moment.

The pastor cleared his throat, snapping me back to the present. I stared at him blankly, then looked back down at Chloe's fingers entwined in mine.

Shock rippled through me as reality sank in. Somehow, I hadn't fully processed until this moment that marrying Chloe meant committing myself fully and unconditionally to her.

Saying 'I do' meant there could be no more London, no more wishing, no more hoping for another chance. This was it. *What on earth are you doing, Todd?* screamed a voice inside my head. *It's literally your last chance. Choose life or death. Get out now!*

For what felt like a long moment, I stood there, paralyzed.

Then, as the pastor moved to reopen his Bible, preparing to read us our vows, my hand darted out and stopped him, resting on the cover of his Bible.

I looked up once more to meet his eyes. "No," I said clearly and surprisingly calmly. He stared at me, wide-eyed and uncomprehending.

"Todd," Chloe whispered, grasping my hand tighter and staring at me with her brow furrowed. "What are you doing?"

I searched her eyes, wishing there were an easier, less painful way. Knowing there wasn't, I answered the only way I could. "What I should have done a long time ago."

I gently released her hand and turned back to face the pastor.

"What are you doing, son?" he repeated her question, uncertainty in his features. I gave him a small smile. "No more lies," I said firmly. I was loud enough that his lapel mic picked up my declaration, broadcasting it throughout the sanctuary. Unsure of what was happening, rustling began to fill the room as our guests murmured speculatively to one another.

For once, there was no sense of caring what everyone thought.

"I have something very important to say," I continued.

"Can it wait?" He looked at Chloe with concern.

"No. It can't."

"Church," he addressed the whispering room. "Before we

proceed with the exchanging of the vows, the groom would like to say a few words." More chatter broke out at his announcement.

"Todd, what are you doing?" Chloe asked again, her face anxious.

I smiled gently at her but didn't answer. Leaving my post, I stepped a few feet to the right and removed the microphone from the wooden podium nearby.

As I loudly cleared my throat, a hush once again came over the room.

"Good afternoon, everyone," I began. As I scanned the crowded church, I couldn't help but notice pretty much every person who'd directed my path and encouraged my growth over the years was present. I gave each of them a nod of acknowledgment as our eyes met.

In the front row, Mom, Sade, and Tena were on the edge of their seats, anxiously staring up at me. Henry and Derek were posted in the back of the church, looking like bodyguards as always.

Khalil was a sentinel a few feet to my left, presumably keeping an eye on Blake, and even Dr. Madison Perry had come out to support me. She sat a few rows back, pinning me with a knowing look. I gave her a small smile in return.

My moment had come, and it felt absolutely right. Here

today, in front of God and all those who had influenced me, I was ready to come clean. For too many years, I had pretended I wanted for myself the same things others wanted for me. But I didn't really want any of those things.

I'd chosen to please others in an attempt to convince myself I was in control. And it nearly meant making the biggest mistake of my life.

"My name is Todd Banks," I started my confession, "and I have been living a lie most of my life." I cut right to the chase. Time was short and I wanted my message to hit home.

"Up until quite recently, life looked pretty good. I even thought I was happy. Now, I can see I was lying to myself, letting others direct me while pretending to be in control. I neither believed in God nor trusted Him to direct my path. Instead, I put my faith in myself and others. I did what I wanted, or so I believed."

I paused to breathe, the room calm and quiet enough to hear a pin drop as everyone waited for my next words with bated breath.

I smiled as I continued. "I convinced myself I wanted what other people wanted for me. But over the past six months, God has shown me the truth. I now know God is not only real, but also very involved in my life. Though I questioned Him, He has answered my prayers repeatedly and some-times very specifically. I even prayed for a sign from God this morning, giving Him a mere thirty minutes to give me concrete proof of His existence. And He did show it to me in a really powerful way."

"Amen!" rang out a voice from the back of the room.

I began to pace the few steps between the bridal party and the wooden podium. "What I'm trying to say is I'm tired of living for everyone else. I'm tired of pretending to be happy when I'm sad. I'm tired of leaving behind my dreams and trying to please other people, even those who don't give a damn about me. And I'm not going to do it any longer."

I turned to face the crowd. "Instead, I'm going to let God lead. Because today, I gave my life to Jesus, and I vowed to trust Him completely."

More shouts of "Amen!" broke out across the room and I was surprised to hear a smattering of applause. Public speaking wasn't really my thing, but apparently my conviction had riled up the room. Thinking I was finished, the pastor stepped forward, extending his hand for the mic, but I shook my head slightly. I wasn't through.

"God has shown me that trusting Him means making choices, sometimes choices that are right, but not necessarily pleasing to everyone else." I glanced over at the bridal party, meeting Khalil's eyes briefly. "Fifteen months ago, I met a woman who changed the entire course of my life. This woman is truly the yin to my yang. And up until just a few hours ago, I thought I had lost her forever."

At this declaration, Chloe's head snapped up. She stared at me, waiting for me to explain further, not wanting to accept what I'd said.

Ignoring the whispers spreading once more throughout the church at my announcement, I set the mic down on the podium and walked the few short steps back to Chloe. I grasped her hands.

As I took in her lovely face, the hurt and heartbreak in her eyes were gut-wrenching. I could easily see how the old me would have caved in to save her from the hurt, prioritizing her needs over mine. But as much as her pain affected me too, without a doubt my truth was elsewhere.

There was only one choice to make.

"I'm sorry, Chloe," I said softly. "You are an amazing woman and you deserve the very best. You deserve someone who loves you wholeheartedly without any reserve. I am sorry, but I am not that man. I cannot marry you. I'm in love with someone else, someone without whom I cannot live. I'm so, so sorry it took me until this moment to realize it."

Over my shoulder came a giant sigh. I turned to see Khalil smiling broadly at me. "Finally!" he said more than a little louder than was polite, reaching up to loosen his tie.

I gave him a quick smile in return.

Releasing Chloe's hands and trying to ignore the tears cascading down her cheeks, I turned and quickly surveyed the room. Those in the pews closest to the front had overheard my confession to Chloe and were frozen in shock, their mouths hanging open.

Farther back, the murmuring whispers had exploded in bursts of curious chatter. Ignoring both, I descended the three steps raising the altar above the congregation.

As I neared the aisle, Chloe's father jumped to his feet. "You no-good bastard!" he exclaimed, heading my way. Before he could reach me, Khalil jumped down the steps and situated himself between us, crossing his arms in front of his chest and looking every bit my bodyguard.

I shot him a grateful look, knowing I'd thank him later.

Feeling the joy bubbling up inside me, I made my way down the aisle and reached the sanctuary doors with a gigantic grin, finally ready to claim my life.

But first, I needed to find the woman of my dreams, again.

A man on a mission, I threw open the double doors and charged through, but didn't make it far. To my surprise, just a few short feet from the entrance to the church stood London, frozen in place and staring at me with a look of sheer incomprehension.

In her hand was the beautiful scarf she'd given me that very first day on the train.

"Thank you, God!" I exclaimed, sending up an impromptu but fervent prayer of gratitude. Smiling at London's surprised look, I made it to her side in two strides, spun her around, threw my arm around her and escorted her toward my car, thankfully parked in the closest row.

As we walked the short distance together, I squeezed her closer to my side, sinking into her sweet smell and soft curves for just a moment. I must have been the luckiest man alive.

Reaching my car, I tucked her into my passenger seat and closed the door gently behind her. Quickly, I made my way to the other side, slipped behind the wheel and threw the car into reverse. Before I pulled out of the spot, I glanced over at London and grinned.

There was a lot of explaining to do, but it was time to start living my life.

Time to live for *me*.